ACCLAIM FOR

Andre Dubus

"Andre Dubus is a master."   —Tobias Wolff

"There isn't a better short story writer in America."
—*Minneapolis Tribune*

"Not since Flannery O'Connor has there been a writer who explores so compellingly the polarities of violence and redemption, anger and tenderness, sexuality and asceticism."   —*Boston Herald*

"His power is ominous and genuine."   —*Vanity Fair*

"More than any writer I can think of, he makes me aware of the simple pleasure of reading a story. . . . Andre Dubus is my hero."
—Elmore Leonard

"His stories are remarkable for their lyricism, for the riches Dubus uncovers in the mundane, and for the enormous generosity of spirit that infuses them."   —*The Plain Dealer*

Andre Dubus

IN THE BEDROOM

The author of nine works of fiction, Andre Dubus received the PEN/Malamud Award, the Rea Award for excellence in short fiction, the Jean Stein Award from the American Academy of Arts and Letters, *The Boston Globe*'s first annual Lawrence L. Winship Award, and fellowships from both the Guggenheim and MacArthur foundations. Until his death in 1999, he lived in Haverhill, Massachusetts.

ALSO BY Andre Dubus

IN THE BEDROOM

· *Seven Stories* ·

Andre Dubus

Preface by Todd Field

VINTAGE CONTEMPORARIES

Vintage Books • A Division of Random House, Inc. • New York

A VINTAGE CONTEMPORARIES ORIGINAL, FEBRUARY 2002

Cataloging-in-Publication Data is available from the Library of Congress.

ISBN: 1-4000-3077-3

Book design by Mia Risberg

www.vintagebooks.com

Printed in the United States of America
10   9   8   7   6

Contents

Preface

Ten years ago I discovered the stories of Andre Dubus. His voice was unique, and yet familiar, like that of a distant male relative. After a time I came to know him, not only through his work, but personally. The last time we spoke was on the day he died—my birthday in 1999.

When Andre first began writing fiction in the 1960s, he turned away from the winking cynicism of his contemporaries, embracing instead the idea of sacrament: writing as a religious act—the relearning and reloving of people as they are and as they might be, and above all the possibility for transcendence. This he achieved so completely that his stories have a resonance few writers have ever attained. He was faithful to the short story and novella. Like Chekhov, he didn't write novels—because he didn't have to. His stories have a lasting power that never leaves you. They bloom like the seeds of a Douglas fir tree—tall, strong, evergreen. His story "Killings" inspired the screenplay for the film *In the Bedroom*, although I know branches from his other stories reached out from that exquisite Dubusian forest and mingled with the script in mysterious ways.

In each of the seven stories collected here, Andre explores the terrain of human desire, disappointment, craziness, lust, and retribution. What does it mean to be a man? What does it mean to be a woman? The big questions. He said that his empathy and curiosity for his female characters came from a desire that began early in life "to understand how my two sisters had to live in the world compared to the way I had to live as a boy." In his story "Rose" you can almost feel him reaching out from the page, embracing this woman as if his life depended upon it.

Before Andre died he sent a couple of new stories to me—Westerns. "I always wanted to write a Western—it's damn near impossible," he said. The characters were in the required attire, and on horseback. But they were Andre's people alright—and could just as easily have been on a lobster boat in Rockland Harbor or parked at a convenience store in the Merrimack Valley—striving and struggling with the same timeless moral issues all of his characters faced.

It is a rare thing to admire an artist from a distance and upon meeting him not be disillusioned. After meeting Andre my admiration for his courage, talent, and humanity grew tenfold. I miss his friendship, and I am grateful to have known him. If you have never read him, get ready—you will never be the same again.

Todd Field

DECEMBER 2001

IN THE BEDROOM

KILLINGS

On the August morning when Matt Fowler buried his youngest
son, Frank, who had lived for twenty-one years, eight months,
and four days, Matt's older son, Steve, turned to him as the family
left the grave and walked between their friends, and said: "I should
kill him." He was twenty-eight, his brown hair starting to thin in
front where he used to have a cowlick. He bit his lower lip, wiped his
eyes, then said it again. Ruth's arm, linked with Matt's, tightened; he
looked at her. Beneath her eyes there was swelling from the three
days she had suffered. At the limousine Matt stopped and looked
back at the grave, the casket, and the Congregationalist minister who
he thought had probably had a difficult job with the eulogy though
he hadn't seemed to, and the old funeral director who was saying
something to the six young pallbearers. The grave was on a hill and
overlooked the Merrimack, which he could not see from where he
stood; he looked at the opposite bank, at the apple orchard with its
symmetrically planted trees going up a hill.

Next day Steve drove with his wife back to Baltimore where he man-
aged the branch office of a bank, and Cathleen, the middle child, drove

with her husband back to Syracuse. They had left the grandchildren with friends. A month after the funeral Matt played poker at Willis Trottier's because Ruth, who knew this was the second time he had been invited, told him to go, he couldn't sit home with her for the rest of her life, she was all right. After the game Willis went outside to tell everyone goodnight and, when the others had driven away, he walked with Matt to his car. Willis was a short, silver-haired man who had opened a diner after World War II, his trade then mostly very early breakfast, which he cooked, and then lunch for the men who worked at the leather and shoe factories. He now owned a large restaurant.

"He walks the Goddamn streets," Matt said.

"I know. He was in my place last night, at the bar. With a girl."

"I don't see him. I'm in the store all the time. Ruth sees him. She sees him too much. She was at Sunnyhurst today getting cigarettes and aspirin, and there he was. She can't even go out for cigarettes and aspirin. It's killing her."

"Come back in for a drink."

Matt looked at his watch. Ruth would be asleep. He walked with Willis back into the house, pausing at the steps to look at the starlit sky. It was a cool summer night; he thought vaguely of the Red Sox, did not even know if they were at home tonight; since it happened he had not been able to think about any of the small pleasures he believed he had earned, as he had earned also what was shattered now forever: the quietly harried and quietly pleasurable days of fatherhood. They went inside. Willis's wife, Martha, had gone to bed hours ago, in the rear of the large house which was rigged with burglar and fire alarms. They went downstairs to the game room: the television set suspended from the ceiling, the pool table, the poker table with beer cans, cards, chips, filled ashtrays, and the six chairs where Matt and his friends had sat, the friends picking up the old banter as though he had only been away on vacation; but he could see the affection and courtesy in their eyes. Willis went behind the bar and mixed them each a Scotch and soda; he stayed behind the bar and looked at Matt sitting on the stool.

"How often have you thought about it?" Willis said.

"Every day since he got out. I didn't think about bail. I thought I wouldn't have to worry about him for years. She sees him all the time. It makes her cry."

"He was in my place a long time last night. He'll be back."

"Maybe he won't."

"The band. He likes the band."

"What's he doing now?"

"He's tending bar up to Hampton Beach. For a friend. Ever notice even the worst bastard always has friends? He couldn't get work in town. It's just tourists and kids up to Hampton. Nobody knows him. If they do, they don't care. They drink what he mixes."

"Nobody tells me about him."

"I hate him, Matt. My boys went to school with him. He was the same then. Know what he'll do? Five at the most. Remember that woman about seven years ago? Shot her husband and dropped him off the bridge in the Merrimack with a hundred pound sack of cement and said all the way through it that nobody helped her. Know where she is now? She's in Lawrence now, a secretary. And whoever helped her, where the hell is he?"

"I've got a .38 I've had for years. I take it to the store now. I tell Ruth it's for the night deposits. I tell her things have changed: we got junkies here now too. Lots of people without jobs. She knows though."

"What does she know?"

"She knows I started carrying it after the first time she saw him in town. She knows it's in case I see him, and there's some kind of a situation—"

He stopped, looked at Willis, and finished his drink. Willis mixed him another.

"What kind of a situation?"

"Where he did something to me. Where I could get away with it."

"How does Ruth feel about that?"

"She doesn't know."

"You said she does, she's got it figured out."

He thought of her that afternoon: when she went into Sunny-hurst, Strout was waiting at the counter while the clerk bagged the things he had bought; she turned down an aisle and looked at soup cans until he left.

"Ruth would shoot him herself, if she thought she could hit him."

"You got a permit?"

"No."

"I do. You could get a year for that."

"Maybe I'll get one. Or maybe I won't. Maybe I'll just stop bring-ing it to the store."

Richard Strout was twenty-six years old, a high school athlete, foot-ball scholarship to the University of Massachusetts where he lasted for almost two semesters before quitting in advance of the final grades that would have forced him not to return. People then said: Dickie can do the work; he just doesn't want to. He came home and did construction work for his father but refused his father's offer to learn the business; his two older brothers had learned it, so that Strout and Sons trucks going about town, and signs on construction sites, now slashed wounds into Matt Fowler's life. Then Richard married a young girl and became a bartender, his salary and tips aug-mented and perhaps sometimes matched by his father, who also posted his bond. So his friends, his enemies (he had those: fist fights or, more often, boys and then young men who had not fought him when they thought they should have), and those who simply knew him by face and name, had a series of images of him which they recalled when they heard of the killing: the high school running back, the young drunk in bars, the oblivious hard-hatted young man eating lunch at a counter, the bartender who could perhaps be called courteous but not more than that: as he tended bar, his dark eyes and dark, wide-jawed face appeared less sullen, near blank.

One night he beat Frank. Frank was living at home and waiting for September, for graduate school in economics, and working as a lifeguard at Salisbury Beach, where he met Mary Ann Strout, in her first month of separation. She spent most days at the beach with her two sons. Before ten o'clock one night Frank came home; he had driven to the hospital first, and he walked into the living room with stitches over his right eye and both lips bright and swollen.

"I'm all right," he said, when Matt and Ruth stood up, and Matt turned off the television, letting Ruth get to him first: the tall, muscled but slender suntanned boy. Frank tried to smile at them but couldn't because of his lips.

"It was her husband, wasn't it?" Ruth said.

"Ex," Frank said. "He dropped in."

Matt gently held Frank's jaw and turned his face to the light, looked at the stitches, the blood under the white of the eye, the bruised flesh.

"Press charges," Matt said.

"No."

"What's to stop him from doing it again? Did you hit him at all? Enough so he won't want to next time?"

"I don't think I touched him."

"So what are you going to do?"

"Take karate," Frank said, and tried again to smile.

"That's not the problem," Ruth said.

"You know you like her," Frank said.

"I like a lot of people. What about the boys? Did they see it?"

"They were asleep."

"Did you leave her alone with him?"

"He left first. She was yelling at him. I believe she had a skillet in her hand."

"Oh for God's sake," Ruth said.

Matt had been dealing with that too: at the dinner table on evenings when Frank wasn't home, was eating with Mary Ann; or, on the other nights—and Frank was with her every night—he talked with Ruth while they watched television, or lay in bed with the windows open and he smelled the night air and imagined, with both pride and muted sorrow, Frank in Mary Ann's arms. Ruth didn't like it because Mary Ann was in the process of divorce, because she had two children, because she was four years older than Frank, and finally—she told this in bed, where she had during all of their marriage told him of her deepest feelings: of love, of passion, of fears about one of the children, of pain Matt had caused her or she had caused him—she was against it because of what she had heard: that the marriage had gone bad early, and for most of it Richard and Mary Ann had both played around.

"That can't be true," Matt said. "Strout wouldn't have stood for it."

"Maybe he loves her."

"He's too hot-tempered. He couldn't have taken that."

But Matt knew Strout had taken it, for he had heard the stories too. He wondered who had told them to Ruth; and he felt vaguely annoyed and isolated: living with her for thirty-one years and still not knowing what she talked about with her friends. On these summer nights he did not so much argue with her as try to comfort her, but finally there was no difference between the two: she had concrete objections, which he tried to overcome. And in his attempt to do this, he neglected his own objections, which were the same as hers, so that as he spoke to her he felt as disembodied as he sometimes did in the store when he helped a man choose a blouse or dress or piece of costume jewelry for his wife.

"The divorce doesn't mean anything," he said. "She was young and maybe she liked his looks and then after a while she realized she was living with a bastard. I see it as a positive thing."

"She's not divorced yet."

"It's the same thing. Massachusetts has crazy laws, that's all. Her age is no problem. What's it matter when she was born? And that other business: even if it's true, which it probably isn't, it's got nothing to do with Frank, it's in the past. And the kids are no problem. She's been married six years; she ought to have kids. Frank likes them. He plays with them. And he's not going to marry her anyway, so it's not a problem of money."

"Then what's he doing with her?"

"She probably loves him, Ruth. Girls always have. Why can't we just leave it at that?"

"He got home at six o'clock Tuesday morning."

"I didn't know you knew. I've already talked to him about it."

Which he had: since he believed almost nothing he told Ruth, he went to Frank with what he believed. The night before, he had followed Frank to the car after dinner.

"You wouldn't make much of a burglar," he said.

"How's that?"

Matt was looking up at him; Frank was six feet tall, an inch and a half taller than Matt, who had been proud when Frank at seventeen outgrew him; he had only felt uncomfortable when he had to reprimand or caution him. He touched Frank's bicep, thought of the young taut passionate body, believed he could sense the desire, and again he felt the pride and sorrow and envy too, not knowing whether he was envious of Frank or Mary Ann.

"When you came in yesterday morning, I woke up. One of these mornings your mother will. And I'm the one who'll have to talk to her. She won't interfere with you. Okay? I know it means—" But he stopped, thinking: I know it means getting up and leaving that suntanned girl and going sleepy to the car, I know—

"Okay," Frank said, and touched Matt's shoulder and got into the car.

There had been other talks, but the only long one was their first one: a night driving to Fenway Park, Matt having ordered the tickets so they could talk, and knowing when Frank said yes, he would go, that he knew the talk was coming too. It took them forty minutes to get to Boston, and they talked about Mary Ann until they joined the city traffic along the Charles River, blue in the late sun. Frank told him all the things that Matt would later pretend to believe when he told them to Ruth.

"It seems like a lot for a young guy to take on," Matt finally said.

"Sometimes it is. But she's worth it."

"Are you thinking about getting married?"

"We haven't talked about it. She can't for over a year. I've got school."

"I *do* like her," Matt said.

He did. Some evenings, when the long summer sun was still low in the sky, Frank brought her home; they came into the house smelling of suntan lotion and the sea, and Matt gave them gin and tonics and started the charcoal in the backyard, and looked at Mary Ann in the lawn chair: long and very light brown hair (Matt thinking that twenty years ago she would have dyed it blonde), and the long brown legs he loved to look at; her face was pretty; she had probably never in her adult life gone unnoticed into a public place. It was in her wide brown eyes that she looked older than Frank; after a few drinks Matt thought what he saw in her eyes was something erotic, testament to the rumors about her; but he knew it wasn't that, or all that: she had, very young, been through a sort of pain that his children, and he and Ruth, had been spared. In the moments of his recognizing that pain, he wanted to tenderly touch her hair, wanted with some gesture to give her solace and hope. And he would glance at Frank, and hope they would love each other, hope Frank would soothe that pain in her heart, take it from her eyes; and her divorce, her age, and her children did not matter at all. On the first two evenings she did not bring her boys, and then Ruth asked her to bring them next time. In bed that night Ruth said, "She hasn't brought them because she's embarrassed. She shouldn't feel embarrassed."

Richard Strout shot Frank in front of the boys. They were sitting on the living room floor watching television, Frank sitting on the couch, and Mary Ann just returning from the kitchen with a tray of sandwiches. Strout came in the front door and shot Frank twice in the chest and once in the face with a 9 mm. automatic. Then he looked at the boys and Mary Ann, and went home to wait for the police.

It seemed to Matt that from the time Mary Ann called weeping to tell him until now, a Saturday night in September, sitting in the car with Willis, parked beside Strout's car, waiting for the bar to close, that he had not so much moved through his life as wandered through it, his spirit like a dazed body bumping into furniture and corners. He had always been a fearful father: when his children were young, at the start of each summer he thought of them drowning in a pond or the sea, and he was relieved when he came home in the evenings and they were there; usually that relief was his only acknowledgment of his fear, which he never spoke of, and which he controlled within his heart. As he had when they were very young and all of them in turn, Cathleen too, were drawn to the high oak in the backyard, and had to climb it. Smiling, he watched them, imagining the fall: and he was poised to catch the small body before it hit the earth. Or his legs were poised; his hands were in his pockets or his arms were folded and, for the child looking down, he appeared relaxed and confident while his heart beat with the two words he wanted to call out but did not: *Don't fall.* In winter he was less afraid: he made sure the ice would hold him before they skated, and he brought or sent them to places where they could sled without ending in the street. So he and his children had survived their childhood, and he only worried about them when he knew they were driving a long distance, and then he lost Frank in a way no father expected to lose his son, and he felt that all the fears he had borne while they were growing up, and all the grief he had been afraid of, had backed up like a huge wave and struck him on the beach and swept him out to sea. Each day he felt the same and when he was able to forget how he felt, when he was able to force himself not to feel that way, the eyes of his clerks and customers defeated him. He wished those eyes were oblivious, even cold; he felt he was withering in their tenderness. And beneath his listless wandering, every day in his soul he shot Richard Strout in the face; while Ruth, going about town on errands, kept seeing him. And at nights in bed she would hold Matt and cry, or sometimes she was silent and Matt would touch her tightening arm, her clenched fist.

As his own right fist was now, squeezing the butt of the revolver, the last of the drinkers having left the bar, talking to each other, going to their separate cars which were in the lot in front of the bar, out of Matt's vision. He heard their voices, their cars, and then the ocean again, across the street. The tide was in and sometimes it smacked the sea wall. Through the windshield he looked at the dark red side wall of the bar, and then to his left, past Willis, at Strout's car, and through its windows he could see the now-emptied parking lot, the road, the sea wall. He could smell the sea.

The front door of the bar opened and closed again and Willis looked at Matt then at the corner of the building; when Strout came around it alone Matt got out of the car, giving up the hope he had kept all night (and for the past week) that Strout would come out with friends, and Willis would simply drive away; thinking: *All right then. All right;* and he went around the front of Willis's car, and at Strout's he stopped and aimed over the hood at Strout's blue shirt ten feet away. Willis was aiming too, crouched on Matt's left, his elbow resting on the hood.

"Mr. Fowler," Strout said. He looked at each of them, and at the guns. "Mr. Trottier."

Then Matt, watching the parking lot and the road, walked quickly between the car and the building and stood behind Strout. He took one leather glove from his pocket and put it on his left hand.

"Don't talk. Unlock the front and back and get in."

Strout unlocked the front door, reached in and unlocked the back, then got in, and Matt slid into the back seat, closed the door with his gloved hand, and touched Strout's head once with the muzzle.

"It's cocked. Drive to your house."

When Strout looked over his shoulder to back the car, Matt aimed at his temple and did not look at his eyes.

"Drive slowly," he said. "Don't try to get stopped."

They drove across the empty front lot and onto the road, Willis's headlights shining into the car; then back through town, the sea wall on the left hiding the beach, though far out Matt could see the ocean; he uncocked the revolver; on the right were the places, most with their neon signs off, that did so much business in summer: the lounges and cafés and pizza houses, the street itself empty of traffic, the way he and Willis had known it would be when they decided to take Strout at the bar rather than knock on his door at two o'clock one morning and risk that one insomniac neighbor. Matt had not told Willis he was afraid he could not be alone with Strout for very long, smell his smells, feel the presence of his flesh, hear his voice, and then shoot him. They left the beach town and then were on the high bridge over the channel: to the left the smacking curling white at the breakwater and beyond that the dark sea and the full moon, and down to his right the small fishing boats bobbing at anchor in the cove. When they left the bridge, the sea was blocked by abandoned beach cottages, and Matt's left hand was sweating in the glove. Out here in the dark in the car he believed Ruth knew. Willis had come to his house at eleven and asked if he wanted a nightcap; Matt went to the bedroom for his wallet, put the gloves in one trouser pocket and the .38 in the other and went back to the living room, his hand in his pocket covering the bulge of the cool cylinder pressed against his fingers, the butt against his palm. When Ruth said goodnight she looked at his face, and he felt she could see in his eyes the gun, and the night he was going to. But he knew he couldn't trust what he saw. Willis's wife had taken her sleeping pill, which gave her eight hours—the reason, Willis had told Matt, he had the alarms installed, for nights when he was late at the restaurant—and when it was all done and Willis got home he would leave ice and a trace of Scotch and soda in two glasses in the game room and tell Martha in the morning that he had left the restaurant early and brought Matt home for a drink.

"He was making it with my wife." Strout's voice was careful, not pleading.

Matt pressed the muzzle against Strout's head, pressed it harder than he wanted to, feeling through the gun Strout's head flinching and moving forward; then he lowered the gun to his lap.

"Don't talk," he said.

Strout did not speak again. They turned west, drove past the Dairy Queen closed until spring, and the two lobster restaurants that faced each other and were crowded all summer and were now also closed, onto the short bridge crossing the tidal stream, and over the engine Matt could hear through his open window the water rushing inland under the bridge; looking to his left he saw its swift moonlit current going back into the marsh which, leaving the bridge, they entered: the salt marsh stretching out on both sides, the grass tall in patches but mostly low and leaning earthward as though windblown, a large dark rock sitting as though it rested on nothing but itself, and shallow pools reflecting the bright moon.

Beyond the marsh they drove through woods, Matt thinking now of the hole he and Willis had dug last Sunday afternoon after telling their wives they were going to Fenway Park. They listened to the game on a transistor radio, but heard none of it as they dug into the soft earth on the knoll they had chosen because elms and maples sheltered it. Already some leaves had fallen. When the hole was deep enough they covered it and the piled earth with dead branches, then cleaned their shoes and pants and went to a restaurant farther up in New Hampshire where they ate sandwiches and drank beer and watched the rest of the game on television. Looking at the back of Strout's head he thought of Frank's grave; he had not been back to it; but he would go before winter, and its second burial of snow.

He thought of Frank sitting on the couch and perhaps talking to the children as they watched television, imagined him feeling young and strong, still warmed from the sun at the beach, and feeling loved, hearing Mary Ann moving about in the kitchen, hearing her walking into the living room; maybe he looked up at her and maybe she said something, looking at him over the tray of sandwiches, smiling at him, saying something the way women do when they offer food as a gift, then the front door opening and this son of a bitch coming in and Frank seeing that he meant the gun in his hand, this son of a bitch and his gun the last person and thing Frank saw on earth.

When they drove into town the streets were nearly empty: a few slow cars, a policeman walking his beat past the darkened fronts of stores. Strout and Matt both glanced at him as they drove by. They were on the main street, and all the stoplights were blinking yellow. Willis and Matt had talked about that too: the lights changed at midnight, so there would be no place Strout had to stop and where he might try to run. Strout turned down the block where he lived and Willis's headlights were no longer with Matt in the back seat. They had planned that too, had decided it was best for just the one car to go to the house, and again Matt had said nothing about his fear of being alone with Strout, especially in his house: a duplex, dark as all the houses on the street were, the street itself lit at the corner of each block. As Strout turned into the driveway Matt thought of the one insomniac neighbor, thought of some man or woman sitting alone in the dark living room, watching the all-night channel from Boston. When Strout stopped the car near the front of the house, Matt said: "Drive it to the back."

He touched Strout's head with the muzzle.

"You wouldn't have it cocked, would you? For when I put on the brakes."

Matt cocked it, and said: "It is now."

Strout waited a moment; then he eased the car forward, the engine doing little more than idling, and as they approached the garage he gently braked. Matt opened the door, then took off the glove and put it in his pocket. He stepped out and shut the door with his hip and said: "All right."

Strout looked at the gun, then got out, and Matt followed him across the grass, and as Strout unlocked the door Matt looked quickly at the row of small backyards on either side, and scattered tall trees, some evergreens, others not, and he thought of the red and yellow leaves on the trees over the hole, saw them falling soon, probably in two weeks, dropping slowly, covering. Strout stepped into the kitchen.

"Turn on the light."

Strout reached to the wall switch, and in the light Matt looked at his wide back, the dark blue shirt, the white belt, the red plaid pants.

"Where's your suitcase?"

"My suitcase?"

"Where is it."

"In the bedroom closet."

"That's where we're going then. When we get to a door you stop and turn on the light."

They crossed the kitchen, Matt glancing at the sink and stove and refrigerator: no dishes in the sink or even the dish rack beside it, no grease splashings on the stove, the refrigerator door clean and white. He did not want to look at any more but he looked quickly at all he could see: in the living room magazines and newspapers in a wicker basket, clean ashtrays, a record player, the records shelved next to it, then down the hall where, near the bedroom door, hung a color photograph of Mary Ann and the two boys sitting on a lawn—there was no house in the picture—Mary Ann smiling at the camera or Strout or whoever held the camera, smiling as she had on Matt's lawn this summer while he waited for the charcoal and they all talked and he looked at her brown legs and at Frank touching her arm, her shoulder, her hair; he moved down the hall with her smile in his mind, wondering: was that when they were both playing around and she was smiling like that at him and they were happy, even sometimes, making it worth it? He recalled her eyes, the pain in them, and he was conscious of the circles of love he was touching with the hand that held the revolver so tightly now as Strout stopped at the door at the end of the hall.

"There's no wall switch."

"Where's the light?"

"By the bed."

"Let's go."

Matt stayed a pace behind, then Strout leaned over and the room was lighted: the bed, a double one, was neatly made; the ashtray on the bedside table clean, the bureau top dustless, and no photographs; probably so the girl—who *was* she?—would not have to see Mary Ann in the bedroom she believed was theirs. But because Matt was a father and a husband, though never an ex-husband, he knew (and did not want to know) that this bedroom had never been theirs alone. Strout turned around; Matt looked at his lips, his wide jaw, and thought of Frank's doomed and fearful eyes looking up from the couch.

"Where's Mr. Trottier?"

"He's waiting. Pack clothes for warm weather."

"What's going on?"

"You're jumping bail."

"Mr. Fowler—"

He pointed the cocked revolver at Strout's face. The barrel trembled but not much, not as much as he had expected. Strout went to the closet and got the suitcase from the floor and opened it on the bed. As he went to the bureau, he said: "He was making it with my wife. I'd go pick up my kids and he'd be there. Sometimes he spent the night. My boys told me."

He did not look at Matt as he spoke. He opened the top drawer and Matt stepped closer so he could see Strout's hands: underwear and socks, the socks rolled, the underwear folded and stacked. He took them back to the bed, arranged them neatly in the suitcase, then from the closet he was taking shirts and trousers and a jacket; he laid them on the bed and Matt followed him to the bathroom and watched from the door while he packed his shaving kit; watched in the bedroom as he folded and packed those things a person accumulated and that became part of him so that at times in the store Matt felt he was selling more than clothes.

"I wanted to try to get together with her again." He was bent over the suitcase. "I couldn't even talk to her. He was always with her. I'm going to jail for it; if I ever get out I'll be an old man. Isn't that enough?"

"You're not going to jail."

Strout closed the suitcase and faced Matt, looking at the gun. Matt went to his rear, so Strout was between him and the lighted hall; then using his handkerchief he turned off the lamp and said: "Let's go."

They went down the hall, Matt looking again at the photograph, and through the living room and kitchen, Matt turning off the lights and talking, frightened that he was talking, that he was telling this lie he had not planned: "It's the trial. We can't go through that, my wife and me. So you're leaving. We've got you a ticket, and a job. A friend of Mr. Trottier's. Out west. My wife keeps seeing you. We can't have that anymore."

Matt turned out the kitchen light and put the handkerchief in his pocket, and they went down the two brick steps and across the lawn. Strout put the suitcase on the floor of the back seat, then got into the front seat and Matt got in the back and put on his glove and shut the door.

"They'll catch me. They'll check passenger lists."

"We didn't use your name."

"They'll figure that out too. You think I wouldn't have done it myself if it was that easy?"

He backed into the street, Matt looking down the gun barrel but not at the profiled face beyond it.

"You were alone," Matt said. "We've got it worked out."

"There's no planes this time of night, Mr. Fowler."

"Go back through town. Then north on 125."

They came to the corner and turned, and now Willis's headlights were in the car with Matt.

"Why north, Mr. Fowler?"

"Somebody's going to keep you for a while. They'll take you to the airport." He uncocked the hammer and lowered the revolver to his lap and said wearily: "No more talking."

As they drove back through town, Matt's body sagged, going limp with his spirit and its new and false bond with Strout, the hope his lie had given Strout. He had grown up in this town whose streets had become places of apprehension and pain for Ruth as she drove and walked, doing what she had to do; and for him too, if only in his mind as he worked and chatted six days a week in his store; he wondered now if his lie would have worked, if sending Strout away would have been enough; but then he knew that just thinking of Strout in Montana or whatever place lay at the end of the lie he had told, thinking of him walking the streets there, loving a girl there (who *was* she?) would be enough to slowly rot the rest of his days. And Ruth's. Again he was certain that she knew, that she was waiting for him.

They were in New Hampshire now, on the narrow highway, passing the shopping center at the state line, and then houses and small stores and sandwich shops. There were few cars on the road. After ten minutes he raised his trembling hand, touched Strout's neck with the gun, and said: "Turn in up here. At the dirt road."

Strout flicked on the indicator and slowed.

"Mr. Fowler?"

"They're waiting here."

Strout turned very slowly, easing his neck away from the gun. In the moonlight the road was light brown, lighter and yellowed where the headlights shone; weeds and a few trees grew on either side of it, and ahead of them were the woods.

"There's nothing back here, Mr. Fowler."

"It's for your car. You don't think we'd leave it at the airport, do you?"

He watched Strout's large, big-knuckled hands tighten on the wheel, saw Frank's face that night: not the stitches and bruised eye and swollen lips, but his own hand gently touching Frank's jaw, turning his wounds to the light. They rounded a bend in the road and were out of sight of the highway: tall trees all around them now, hiding the moon. When they reached the abandoned gravel pit on the left, the bare flat earth and steep pale embankment behind it, and the black crowns of trees at its top, Matt said: "Stop here."

Strout stopped but did not turn off the engine. Matt pressed the gun hard against his neck, and he straightened in the seat and looked in the rearview mirror, Matt's eyes meeting his in the glass for an instant before looking at the hair at the end of the gun barrel.

"Turn it off."

Strout did, then held the wheel with two hands, and looked in the mirror.

"I'll do twenty years, Mr. Fowler; at least. I'll be forty-six years old."

"That's nine years younger than I am," Matt said, and got out and took off the glove and kicked the door shut. He aimed at Strout's ear and pulled back the hammer. Willis's headlights were off and Matt heard him walking on the soft thin layer of dust, the hard earth beneath it. Strout opened the door, sat for a moment in the interior light, then stepped out onto the road. Now his face was pleading. Matt did not look at his eyes, but he could see it in the lips.

"Just get the suitcase. They're right up the road."

Willis was beside him now, to his left. Strout looked at both guns. Then he opened the back door, leaned in, and with a jerk brought the suitcase out. He was turning to face them when Matt said: "Just walk up the road. Just ahead."

Strout turned to walk, the suitcase in his right hand, and Matt and Willis followed; as Strout cleared the front of his car he dropped the suitcase and, ducking, took one step that was the beginning of a sprint to his right. The gun kicked in Matt's hand, and the explosion of the shot surrounded him, isolated him in a nimbus of sound that cut him off from all his time, all his history, isolated him standing absolutely still on the dirt road with the gun in his hand, looking down at Richard Strout squirming on his belly, kicking one leg behind him, pushing himself forward, toward the woods. Then Matt went to him and shot him once in the back of the head.

Driving south to Boston, wearing both gloves now, staying in the middle lane and looking often in the rearview mirror at Willis's headlights, he relived the suitcase dropping, the quick dip and turn of Strout's back, and the kick of the gun, the sound of the shot. When he walked to Strout, he still existed within the first shot, still trembled and breathed with it. The second shot and the burial seemed to be happening to someone else, someone he was watching. He and Willis each held an arm and pulled Strout face-down off the road and into the woods, his bouncing sliding belt white under the trees where it was so dark that when they stopped at the top of the knoll, panting and sweating, Matt could not see where Strout's blue shirt ended and the earth began. They pulled off the branches then dragged Strout to the edge of the hole and went behind him and lifted his legs and pushed him in. They stood still for a moment. The woods were quiet save for their breathing, and Matt remembered hearing the movements of birds and small animals after the first shot. Or maybe he had not heard them. Willis went down to the road. Matt could see him clearly out on the tan dirt, could see the glint of Strout's car and, beyond the road, the gravel pit. Willis came back up the knoll with the suitcase. He dropped it in the hole and took off his gloves and they went down to his car for the spades. They worked quietly. Sometimes they paused to listen to the woods. When they were finished Willis turned on his flashlight and they covered the earth with leaves and branches and then went down to the spot in front of the car, and while Matt held the light Willis crouched and sprinkled dust on the blood, backing up till he reached the grass and leaves, then he used leaves until they had worked up to the grave again. They did not stop. They walked around the grave and through the woods, using the light on the ground, looking up through the trees to where they ended at the lake. Neither of them spoke above the sounds of their heavy and clumsy strides through low brush and over fallen branches. Then they reached it: wide and dark, lapping softly at the bank, pine needles smooth under Matt's feet, moonlight on the lake, a small island near its middle, with black, tall evergreens. He took out the gun and threw for the island: taking two steps back on the pine needles, striding with the throw and going to one knee as he followed through, looking up to see the dark shapeless object arcing downward, splashing.

They left Strout's car in Boston, in front of an apartment building on Commonwealth Avenue. When they got back to town Willis drove slowly over the bridge and Matt threw the keys into the Merrimack. The sky was turning light. Willis let him out a block from his house, and walking home he listened for sounds from the houses he passed. They were quiet. A light was on in his living room. He turned it off and undressed in there, and went softly toward the bedroom; in the hall he smelled the smoke, and he stood in the bedroom doorway and looked at the orange of her cigarette in the dark. The curtains were closed. He went to the closet and put his shoes on the floor and felt for a hanger.

"Did you do it?" she said.

He went down the hall to the bathroom and in the dark he washed his hands and face. Then he went to her, lay on his back, and pulled the sheet up to his throat.

"Are you all right?" she said.

"I think so."

Now she touched him, lying on her side, her hand on his belly, his thigh.

"Tell me," she said.

He started from the beginning, in the parking lot at the bar; but soon with his eyes closed and Ruth petting him, he spoke of Strout's house: the order, the woman presence, the picture on the wall.

"The way she was smiling," he said.

"What about it?"

"I don't know. Did you ever see Strout's girl? When you saw him in town?"

"No."

"I wonder who she was."

Then he thought: *not was: is. Sleeping now she is his girl.* He opened his eyes, then closed them again. There was more light beyond the curtains. With Ruth now he left Strout's house and told again his lie to Strout, gave him again that hope that Strout must have for a while believed, else he would have to believe only the gun pointed at him for the last two hours of his life. And with Ruth he saw again the dropping suitcase, the darting move to the right: and he told of the first shot, feeling her hand on him but his heart isolated still, beating on the road still in that explosion like thunder. He told her the rest, but the words had no images for him, he did not see himself doing what the words said he had done; he only saw himself on that road.

"We can't tell the other kids," she said. "It'll hurt them, thinking he got away. But we mustn't."

"No."

She was holding him, wanting him, and he wished he could make love with her but he could not. He saw Frank and Mary Ann making love in her bed, their eyes closed, their bodies brown and smelling of the sea; the other girl was faceless, bodiless, but he felt her sleeping now; and he saw Frank and Strout, their faces alive; he saw red and yellow leaves falling to the earth, then snow: falling and freezing and falling; and holding Ruth, his cheek touching her breast, he shuddered with a sob that he kept silent in his heart.

THE WINTER FATHER

for Pat

The Jackman's marriage had been adulterous and violent, but in its last days, they became a couple again, as they might have if one of them were slowly dying. They wept together, looked into each other's eyes without guile, distrust, or hatred, and they planned Peter's time with the children. On his last night at home, he and Norma, tenderly, without a word, made love. Next evening, when he got home from Boston, they called David and Kathi in from the snow and brought them to the kitchen.

David was eight, slender, with light brown hair nearly to his shoulders, a face that was still pretty; he seemed always hungry, and Peter liked watching him eat. Kathi was six, had long red hair and a face that Peter had fallen in love with, a face that had once been pierced by glass the shape of a long dagger blade. In early spring a year ago: he still had not taken the storm windows off the screen doors; he was bringing his lunch to the patio, he did not know Kathi was following him, and holding his plate and mug he had pushed the door open with his shoulder, stepped outside, heard the crash and her scream, and turned to see her gripping then pulling the long shard from her cheek. She got it out before he reached her. He picked her up and pressed his handkerchief to the wound, midway between her eye and throat, and held her as he phoned his doctor who said he would meet them at the hospital and do the stitching himself because it was cosmetic and that beautiful face should not be touched by residents. Norma was not at home. Kathi lay on the car seat beside him and he held his handkerchief on her cheek, and in the hospital he held her hands while she lay on the table. The doctor said it would only take about four stitches and it would be better without anesthetic, because sometimes that puffed the skin, and he wanted to fit the cut together perfectly, for the scar; he told this very gently to Kathi, and he said as she grew, the scar would move down her face and finally would be under her jaw. Then she and Peter squeezed each other's hands as the doctor stitched and she gritted her teeth and stared at pain.

She was like that when he and Norma told them. It was David who suddenly cried, begged them not to get a divorce, and then fled to his room and would not come out, would not help Peter load his car, and only emerged from the house as Peter was driving away: a small running shape in the dark, charging the car, picking up something and throwing it, missing, crying *You bum You bum You bum . . .*

Drunk that night in his apartment whose rent he had paid and keys received yesterday morning before last night's grave lovemaking with Norma, he gained through the blur of bourbon an intense focus on his children's faces as he and Norma spoke: We fight too much, we've tried to live together but can't; you'll see, you'll be better off too, you'll be with Daddy for dinner on Wednesday nights, and on Saturdays and Sundays you'll do things with him. In his kitchen he watched their faces.

Next day he went to the radio station. After the news at noon he was on; often, as the records played, he imagined his children last night, while he and Norma were talking, and after he was gone. Perhaps she took them out to dinner, let them stay up late, flanking her on the couch in front of the television. When he talked he listened to his voice: it sounded as it did every weekday afternoon. At four he was finished. In the parking lot he felt as though, with stooped shoulders, he were limping. He started the forty-minute drive northward, for the first time in twelve years going home to empty rooms. When he reached the town where he lived he stopped at a small store and bought two lamb chops and a package of frozen peas. *I will take one thing at a time*, he told himself. Crossing the sidewalk to his car, in that short space, he felt the limp again, the stooped shoulders. He wondered if he looked like a man who had survived an accident which had killed others.

That was on a Thursday. When he woke Saturday morning, his first thought was a wish: that Norma would phone and tell him they were sick, and he should wait to see them Wednesday. He amended his wish, lay waiting for his own body to let him know it was sick, out for the weekend. In late morning he drove to their coastal town; he had moved fifteen miles inland. Already the snow-ploughed streets and country roads leading to their house felt like parts of his body: intestines, lung, heart-fiber lying from his door to theirs. When they were born he had smoked in the waiting room with the others. Now he was giving birth: stirruped, on his back, waves of pain. There would be no release, no cutting of the cord. Nor did he want it. He wanted to grow a cord.

Walking up their shovelled walk and ringing the doorbell, he felt at the same time like an inept salesman and a con man. He heard their voices, watched the door as though watching the sounds he heard, looking at the point where their faces would appear, but when the door opened he was looking at Norma's waist; then up to her face, lipsticked, her short brown hair soft from that morning's washing. For years she had not looked this way on a Saturday morning. Her eyes held him: the nest of pain was there, the shyness, the coiled anger; but there was another shimmer: she was taking a new marriage vow: This is the way we shall love our children now; watch how well I can do it. She smiled and said: "Come in out of the cold and have a cup of coffee."

In the living room he crouched to embrace the hesitant children. Only their faces were hesitant. In his arms they squeezed, pressed, kissed. David's hard arms absolved them both of Wednesday night. Through their hair Peter said pleasantly to Norma that he'd skip the coffee this time. Grabbing caps and unfurling coats, they left the house, holding hands to the car.

He showed them his apartment: they had never showered behind glass; they slid the doors back and forth. Sand washing down the drain, their flesh sunburned, a watermelon waiting in the refrigerator . . .

"This summer—"

They turned from the glass, looked up at him.

"When we go to the beach. We can come back here and shower."

Their faces reflected his bright promise, and they followed him to the kitchen; on the counter were two cans of kidney beans, Jalapeño peppers, seasonings. Norma kept her seasonings in small jars, and two years ago when David was six and came home bullied and afraid of next day at school, Peter asked him if the boy was bigger than he was, and when David said "A lot," and showed him the boy's height with one hand, his breadth with two, Peter took the glass stopper from the cinnamon jar, tied it in a handkerchief corner, and struck his palm with it, so David would know how hard it was, would believe in it. Next morning David took it with him. On the school-ground, when the bully shoved him, he swung it up from his back pocket and down on the boy's forehead. The boy cried and went away. After school David found him on the sidewalk and hit his jaw with the weapon he had sat on all day, chased him two blocks swinging at his head, and came home with delighted eyes, no damp traces of yesterday's shame and fright, and Peter's own pain and rage turned to pride, then caution, and he spoke gently, told David to carry it for a week or so more, but not to use it unless the bully attacked; told him we must control our pleasure in giving pain.

Now reaching into the refrigerator he felt the children behind him; then he knew it was not them he felt, for in the bathroom when he spoke to their faces he had also felt a presence to his rear, watching, listening. It was the walls, it was fatherhood, it was himself. He was not an early drinker but he wanted an ale now; looked at the brown bottles long enough to fear and dislike his reason for wanting one, then he poured two glasses of apple cider and, for himself, cider and club soda. He sat at the table and watched David slice a Jalapeño over the beans, and said: "Don't ever touch one of those and take a leak without washing your hands first."

"Why?"

"I did it once. Think about it."

"Wow."

They talked of flavors as Kathi, with her eyes just above rim-level of the pot, her wrists in the steam, poured honey, and shook paprika, basil, parsley, Worcestershire, wine vinegar. In a bowl they mixed ground meat with a raw egg: jammed their hands into it, fingers touching; scooped and squeezed meat and onion and celery between their fingers; the kitchen smelled of bay leaf in the simmering beans, and then of broiling meat. They talked about the food as they ate, pressing thick hamburgers to fit their mouths, and only then Peter heard the white silence coming at them like afternoon snow. They cleaned the counter and table and what they had used; and they spoke briefly, quietly, they smoothly passed things; and when Peter turned off the faucet, all sound stopped, the kitchen was multiplied by silence, the apartment's walls grew longer, the floors wider, the ceilings higher. Peter walked the distance to his bedroom, looked at his watch, then quickly turned to the morning paper's television listing, and called: "Hey! *The Magnificent Seven*'s coming on."

"All *right*," David said, and they hurried down the short hall, light footsteps whose sounds he could name: Kathi's, David's, Kathi's. He lay between them, bellies down, on the bed.

"Is this our third time or fourth?" Kathi said.

"I think our fourth. We saw it in a theater once."

"I could see it every week," David said.

"Except when Charles Bronson dies," Kathi said. "But I like when the little kids put flowers on his grave. And when he spanks them."

The winter sunlight beamed through the bedroom window, the afternoon moving past him and his children. Driving them home he imitated Yul Brynner, Eli Wallach, Charles Bronson; the children praised his voices, laughed, and in front of their house they kissed him and asked what they were going to do tomorrow. He said he didn't know yet; he would call in the morning, and he watched them go up the walk between snow as high as Kathi's waist. At the door they turned and waved; he tapped the horn twice, and drove away.

That night he could not sleep. He read *Macbeth*, woke propped against the pillows, the bedside lamp on, the small book at his side. He put it on the table, turned out the light, moved the pillows down, and slept. Next afternoon he took David and Kathi to a movie.

He did not bring them to his apartment again, unless they were on the way to another place, and their time in the apartment was purposeful and short: Saturday morning cartoons, then lunch before going to a movie or museum. Early in the week he began reading the movie section of the paper, looking for matinees. Every weekend they went to a movie, and sometimes two, in their towns and other small towns and in Boston. On the third Saturday he took them to a PG movie which was bloody and erotic enough to make him feel ashamed and irresponsible as he sat between his children in the theater. Driving home, he asked them about the movie until he believed it had not frightened them, or made them curious about bodies and urges they did not yet have. After that, he saw all PG movies before taking them, and he was angry at mothers who left their children at the theater and picked them up when the movie was over; and left him to listen to their children exclaiming at death, laughing at love; and often they roamed the aisles going to the concession stand, and distracted him from this weekly entertainment which he suspected he waited for and enjoyed more than David and Kathi. He had not been an indiscriminate moviegoer since he was a child. Now what had started as a duty was pleasurable, relaxing. He knew that beneath this lay a base of cowardice. But he told himself it would pass. A time would come when he and Kathi and David could sit in his living room, talking like three friends who had known each other for eight and six years.

Most of his listeners on weekday afternoons were women. Between love songs he began talking to them about movie ratings. He said not to trust them. He asked what they felt about violence and sex in movies, whether or not they were bad for children. He told them he didn't know; that many of the fairy tales and all the comic books of his boyhood were violent; and so were the Westerns and serials on Saturday afternoons. But there was no blood. And he chided the women about letting their children go to the movies alone.

He got letters and read them in his apartment at night. Some thanked him for his advice about ratings. Many told him it was all right for him to talk, he wasn't with the kids every afternoon after school and all weekends and holidays and summer; the management of the theater was responsible for quiet and order during the movies; they were showing the movies to attract children and they were glad to take the money. The children came home happy and did not complain about other children being noisy. Maybe he should stop going to matinees, should leave his kids there and pick them up when it was over. *It's almost what I'm doing*, he thought; and he stopped talking about movies to the afternoon women.

He found a sledding hill: steep and long, and at its base a large frozen pond. David and Kathi went with him to buy his sled, and with a thermos of hot chocolate they drove to the hill near his apartment. Parked cars lined the road, and children and some parents were on the hill's broad top. Red-faced children climbed back, pulling their sleds with ropes. Peter sledded first; he knew the ice on the pond was safe, but he was beginning to handle fatherhood as he did guns: always as if they were loaded, when he knew they were not. There was a satisfaction in preventing even dangers which did not exist.

The snow was hard and slick, rushed beneath him; he went over a bump, rose from the sled, nearly lost it, slammed down on it, legs outstretched, gloved hands steering around the next bump but not the next one suddenly rising toward his face, and he pressed against the sled, hugged the wood-shock to his chest, yelled with delight at children moving slowly upward, hit the edge of the pond and sledded straight out, looking at the evergreens on its far bank. The sled stopped near the middle of the pond; he stood and waved to the top of the hill, squinting at sun and bright snow, then two silhouettes waved back and he saw Kathi's long red hair. Holding the sled's rope he walked on ice, moving to his left as David started down and Kathi stood waiting, leaning on her sled. He told himself he was a fool: had lived winters with his children, yet this was the first sled he had bought for himself; sometimes he had gone with them because they asked him to, and he had used their sleds. But he had never found a sledding hill. He had driven past them, seen the small figures on their crests and slopes, but no more. Watching David swerve around a bump and Kathi, at the top, pushing her sled, then dropping onto it, he forgave himself; there was still time; already it had begun.

But on that first afternoon of sledding he made a mistake: within an hour his feet were painfully cold, his trousers wet and his legs cold; David and Kathi wore snow pants. Beneath his parka he was sweating. Then he knew they felt the same, yet they would sled as long as he did, because of the point and edges of divorce that pierced and cut all their time together.

"I'm freezing," he said. "I can't move my toes."

"Me too," David said.

"Let's go down one more time," Kathi said.

Then he took them home. It was only three o'clock.

After that he took them sledding on weekend mornings. They brought clothes with them, and after sledding they went to his apartment and showered. They loved the glass doors. On the first day they argued about who would shower first, until Peter flipped a coin and David won and Peter said Kathi would have the first shower next time and they would take turns that way. They showered long and when Peter's turn came the water was barely warm and he was quickly in and out. Then in dry clothes they ate lunch and went to a movie.

Or to another place, and one night drinking bourbon in his living room, lights off so he could watch the snow falling, the yellowed, gentle swirl at the corner streetlight, the quick flakes at his window, banking on the sill, and across the street the grey-white motion lowering the sky and making the evergreens look distant, he thought of owning a huge building to save divorced fathers. Free admission. A place of swimming pool, badminton and tennis courts, movie theaters, restaurants, soda fountains, batting cages, a zoo, an art gallery, a circus, aquarium, science museum, hundreds of restrooms, two always in sight, everything in the tender charge of women trained in first aid and Montessori, no uniforms, their only style warmth and cheer. A father could spend entire days there, weekend after weekend, so in winter there would not be all this planning and driving. He had made his cowardice urbane, mobile, and sophisticated; but perhaps at its essence cowardice knows it is apparent: he believed David and Kathi knew that their afternoons at the aquarium, the Museum of Fine Arts, the Science Museum, were houses Peter had built, where they could be together as they were before, with one difference: there was always entertainment.

Frenetic as they were, he preferred weekends to the Wednesday nights when they ate together. At first he thought it was shyness. Yet they talked easily, often about their work, theirs at school, his as a disc jockey. When he was not with the children he spent much time thinking about what they said to each other. And he saw that, in his eight years as a father, he had been attentive, respectful, amusing; he had taught and disciplined. But no: not now: when they were too loud in the car or they fought, he held onto his anger, his heart buffeted with it, and spoke calmly, as though to another man's children, for he was afraid that if he scolded as he had before, the day would be spoiled, they would not have the evening at home, the sleeping in the same house, to heal them; and they might not want to go with him next day or two nights from now or two days. During their eight and six years with him, he had shown them love, and made them laugh. But now he knew that he had remained a secret from them. What did they know about him? What did he know about them?

He would tell them about his loneliness, and what he had learned about himself. When he wasn't with them, he was lonely all the time, except while he was running or working, and sometimes at the station he felt it waiting for him in the parking lot, on the highway, in his apartment. He thought much about it, like an athletic man considering a sprained ligament, changing his exercises to include it. He separated his days into parts, thought about each one, and learned that all of them were not bad. When the alarm woke him in the winter dark, the new day and waiting night were the grey of the room, and they pressed down on him, fetid repetitions bent on smothering his spirit before he rose from the bed. But he got up quickly, made the bed while the sheets still held his warmth, and once in the kitchen with coffee and newspaper he moved into the first part of the day: bacon smell and solemn disc jockeys with classical music, an hour or more at the kitchen table, as near-peaceful as he dared hope for, and was grateful for too, as it went with him to the living room, to the chair at the southeast window where, pausing to watch traffic and look at the snow and winter branches of elms and maples in the park across the street, he sat in sun-warmth and entered the cadence of Shakespeare. In mid-morning, he Vaselined his face and genitals and, wearing layers of nylon, he ran two and a half miles down the road which, at his corner, was a town road of close houses but soon was climbing and dropping past farms and meadows; at the crest of a hill, where he could see the curves of trees on the banks of the Merrimack, he turned and ran back.

The second part began with ignition and seat belt, driving forty minutes on the highway, no buildings or billboards, low icicled cliffs and long white hills, and fields and woods in the angled winter sun, and in the silent car he received his afternoon self: heard the music he had chosen, popular music he would not listen to at home but had come to accept and barely listen to at work, heard his voice in mime and jest and remark, often merry, sometimes showing off and knowing it, but not much, no more than he had earned. That part of his day behind glass and microphone, with its comfort drawn from combining the familiar with the spontaneous, took him to four o'clock.

The next four hours, he learned, were not only the time he had to prepare for, but also the lair of his loneliness, the source of every quick chill of loss, each sudden whisper of dread and futility: for if he could spend them with a woman he loved, drink and cook and eat with her while day changed to night (though now, in winter, night came as he drove home), he and this woman huddled in the light and warmth of living room and kitchen, gin and meat, then his days until four and nights after eight would demand less from him of will, give more to him of hopeful direction. After dinner he listened to jazz and read fiction or watched an old movie on television until, without lust or even the need of a sleeping woman beside him, he went to bed: a blessing, but a disturbing one. He had assumed, as a husband and then an adulterous one, that his need for a woman was as carnal as it was spiritual. But now celibacy was easy; when he imagined a woman, she was drinking with him, eating dinner. So his most intense and perhaps his only need for a woman was then; and all the reasons for the end of his marriage became distant, blurred, and he wondered if the only reason he was alone now was a misogyny he had never recognized: that he did not even want a woman except at the day's end, and had borne all the other hours of woman-presence only to have her comfort as the clock's hands moved through their worst angles of the day.

Planning to tell all this to David and Kathi, knowing he would need gin to do it, he was frightened, already shy as if they sat with him now in the living room. A good sign: if he were afraid, then it took courage; if it took courage, then it must be right. He drank more bourbon than he thought he did, and went to bed excited by intimacy and love.

He slept off everything. In the morning he woke so amused at himself that, if he had not been alone, he would have laughed aloud. He imagined telling his children, over egg rolls and martinis and Shirley Temples, about his loneliness and his rituals to combat it. And *that* would be his new fatherhood, smelling of duck sauce and hot mustard and gin. Swallowing aspirins and orange juice, he saw clearly why he and the children were uncomfortable together, especially at Wednesday night dinners: when he lived with them, their talk had usually dealt with the immediate (I don't like playing with Cindy anymore; she's too bossy. I wish it would snow; it's no use being cold if it doesn't snow); they spoke at dinner and breakfast and, during holidays and summer, at lunch; in the car and stores while running errands; on the summer lawn while he prepared charcoal; and in their beds when he went to tell them goodnight; most of the time their talk was deep only because it was affectionate and tribal, sounds made between creatures sharing the same blood. Now their talk was the same, but it did not feel the same. They talked in his car and in places he took them, and the car and each place would not let them forget they were there because of divorce.

So their talk had felt evasive, fragile, contrived, and his drunken answer last night had been more talk: courageous, painful, honest. *My God*, he thought, as in a light snow that morning he ran out of his hangover, into lucidity. *I was going to have a Goddamn therapy session with my own children.* Breathing the smell of new snow and winter air he thought of this fool Peter Jackman, swallowing his bite of pork fried rice, and saying: And what do you feel at school? About the divorce, I mean. Are you ashamed around the other kids? He thought of the useless reopening and sometimes celebrating of wounds he and Norma had done with the marriage counselor, a pleasant and smart woman, but what could she do when all she had to work with was wounds? After each session he and Norma had driven home, usually mute, always in despair. Then, running faster, he imagined a house where he lived and the children came on Friday nights and stayed all weekend, played with their friends during the day, came and left the house as they needed, for food, drink, bathroom, diversion, and at night they relaxed together as a family; saw himself reading as they painted and drew at the kitchen table . . .

That night they ate dinner at a seafood restaurant thirty minutes from their town. When he drove them home he stayed outside their house for a while, the three of them sitting in front for warmth; they talked about summer and no school and no heavy clothes and no getting up early when it was still dark outside. He told them it was his favorite season too because of baseball and the sea. Next morning when he got into his car, the inside of his windshield was iced. He used the small plastic scraper from his glove compartment. As he scraped the middle and right side, he realized the grey ice curling and falling from the glass was the frozen breath of his children.

At a bar in the town where his children lived, he met a woman. This was on a Saturday night, after he had taken them home from the Museum of Fine Arts. They had liked Monet and Cézanne, had shown him light and color they thought were pretty. He told them Cézanne's *The Turn in the Road* was his favorite, that every time he came here he stood looking at it and he wanted to be walking up that road, toward the houses. But all afternoon he had known they were restless. They had not sledded that morning. Peter had gone out drinking the night before, with his only married friend who could leave his wife at home without paying even a subtle price, and he had slept through the time for sledding, had apologized when they phoned and woke him, and on the drive to the museum had told them he and Sibley (whom they knew as a friend of their mother too) had been having fun and had lost track of time until the bar closed. So perhaps they wanted to be outdoors. Or perhaps it was the old resonance of place again, the walls and ceiling of the museum, even the paintings telling them: You are here because your father left home.

He went to the bar for a sandwich, and stayed. Years ago he had come here often, on the way home from work, or at night with Norma. It was a neighborhood bar then, where professional fishermen and lobstermen and other men who worked with their hands drank, and sometimes brought their wives. Then someone from Boston bought it, put photographs and drawings of fishing and pleasure boats on the walls, built a kitchen which turned out quiche and crêpes, hired young women to tend the bar, and musicians to play folk and bluegrass. The old customers left. The new ones were couples and people trying to be a couple for at least the night, and that is why Peter stayed after eating his sandwich.

Within an hour she came in and sat at the bar, one empty chair away from him: a woman in her late twenties, dark eyes and light brown hair. Soon they were talking. He liked her because she smiled a lot. He also liked her drink: Jack Daniel's on the rocks. Her name was Mary Ann; her last name kept eluding him. She was a market researcher, and like many people Peter knew, she seemed to dismiss her work, though she was apparently good at it; her vocation was recreation: she skied down and across; backpacked; skated; camped; ran and swam. He began to imagine doing things with her, and he felt more insidious than if he were imagining passion: he saw her leading him and Kathi and David up a mountain trail. He told her he spent much of his life prone or sitting, except for a daily five-mile run, a habit from the Marine Corps (she gave him the sneer and he said: Come on, that was a long time ago, it was peacetime, it was fun), and he ran now for the same reasons everyone else did, or at least everyone he knew who ran: the catharsis, which kept his body feeling good, and his mind more or less sane. He said he had not slept in a tent since the Marines; probably because of the Marines. He said he wished he did as many things as she did, and he told her why. Some time in his bed during the night, she said: "They probably did like the paintings. At least you're not taking them to all those movies now."

"We still go about once a week."

"Did you know Lennie's has free matinees for children? On Sunday afternoons?"

"No."

"I have a divorced friend; she takes her kids almost every Sunday."

"Why don't we go tomorrow?"

"With your kids?"

"If you don't mind."

"Sure. I like kids. I'd like to have one of my own, without a husband."

As he kissed her belly he imagined her helping him pitch the large tent he would buy, the four of them on a weekend of cold brook and trees on a mountainside, a fire, bacon in the skillet . . .

In the morning he scrambled their eggs, then phoned Norma. He had a general dislike of telephones: talking to his own hand gripping plastic, pacing, looking about the room; the timing of hanging up was tricky. Nearly all these conversations left him feeling as disconnected as the phone itself. But talking with Norma was different: he marvelled at how easy it was. The distance and disembodiment he felt on the phone with others were good here. He and Norma had hurt each other deeply, and their bodies had absorbed the pain: it was the stomach that tightened, the hands that shook, the breast that swelled then shrivelled. Now fleshless they could talk by phone, even with warmth, perhaps alive from the time when their bodies were at ease together. He thought of having a huge house where he could live with his family, seeing Norma only at meals, shared for the children, he and Norma talking to David and Kathi; their own talk would be on extension phones in their separate wings: they would discuss the children, and details of running the house. This was of course the way they had finally lived, without the separate wings, the phones. And one of their justifications as they talked of divorce was that the children would be harmed, growing up in a house with parents who did not love each other, who rarely touched, and then by accident. There had been moments near the end when, brushing against each other in the kitchen, one of them would say: Sorry. Now as Mary Ann Brighi (he had waked knowing her last name) spread jam on toast, he phoned.

"I met this woman last night."

Mary Ann smiled; Norma's voice did.

"It's about time. I was worried about your arm going."

"What about you?"

"I'm doing all right."

"Do you bring them home?"

"It's not them, and I get a sitter."

"But he comes to the house? To take you out?"

"Peter?"

"What."

"What are we talking about?"

"I was wondering what the kids would think if Mary Ann came along this afternoon."

"What they'll think is Mary Ann's coming along this afternoon."

"You're sure that's all?"

"Unless you fuck in front of them."

He turned his face from Mary Ann, but she had already seen his blush; he looked at her smiling with toast crumbs on her teeth. He wished he were married and lovemaking were simple. But after cleaning the kitchen he felt passion again, though not much; in his mind he was introducing the children to Mary Ann. He would make sure he talked to them, did not leave them out while he talked to her. He was making love while he thought this; he hoped they would like her; again he saw them hiking up a trail through pines, stopping for Kathi and David to rest; a sudden bounding deer; the camp beside the stream; he thanked his member for doing its work down there while the rest of him was in the mountains in New Hampshire.

As he walked with David and Kathi he held their hands; they were looking at her face watching them from the car window.

"She's a new friend of mine," he said. "Just a friend. She wants to show us this night club where children can go on Sunday afternoons."

From the back seat they shook hands, peered at her, glanced at Peter, their eyes making him feel that like adults they could sense when people were lovers; he adjusted the rearview mirror, watched their faces, decided he was seeing jumbled and vulnerable curiosity: Who was she? Would she marry their father? Would they like her? Would their mother be sad? And the night club confused them.

"Isn't that where people go drink?" Kathi said.

"It's afternoon too," David said.

Not for Peter; the sky was grey, the time was grey, dark was coming, and all at once he felt utterly without will; all the strength he had drawn on to be with his children left him like one long spurt of arterial blood: all his time with his children was grey, with night coming; it would always be; nothing would change: like three people cursed in an old myth they would forever be thirty-three and eight and six, in this car on slick or salted roads, going from one place to another. He disapproved of but understood those divorced fathers who fled to live in a different pain far away. Beneath his despair, he saw himself and his children sledding under a lovely blue sky, heard them laughing in movies, watching in awe like love a circling blue shark in the aquarium's tank; but these seemed beyond recapture.

He entered the highway going south, and that quick transition of hands and head and eyes as he moved into fast traffic snapped him out of himself, into the sound of Mary Ann's voice: with none of the rising and falling rhythm of nursery talk, she was telling them, as if speaking to a young man and woman she had just met, about Lennie's. How Lennie believed children should hear good music, not just the stuff on the radio. She talked about jazz. She hummed some phrases of "Somewhere Over the Rainbow," then improvised. They would hear Gerry Mulligan today, she said, and as she talked about the different saxophones, Peter looked in the mirror at their listening faces.

"And Lennie has a cook from Tijuana in Mexico," Mary Ann said. "She makes the best chili around."

Walking into Lennie's with a pretty woman and his two healthy and pretty children, he did not feel like a divorced father looking for something to do; always in other places he was certain he looked that way, and often he felt guilty when talking with waitresses. He paid the cover charge for himself and Mary Ann and she said: All right, but I buy the first two rounds, and he led her and the children to a table near the bandstand. He placed the children between him and Mary Ann. Bourbon, Cokes, bowls of chili. The room was filling and Peter saw that at most tables there were children with parents, usually one parent, usually a father. He watched his children listening to Mulligan. His fingers tapped the table with the drummer. He looked warmly at Mary Ann's profile until she turned and smiled at him.

Often Mulligan talked to the children, explained how his saxophone worked; his voice was cheerful, joking, never serious, as he talked about the guitar and bass and piano and drums. He clowned laughter from the children in the dark. Kathi and David turned to each other and Peter to share their laughter. During the music they listened intently. Their hands tapped the table. They grinned at Peter and Mary Ann. At intermission Mulligan said he wanted to meet the children. While his group went to the dressing room he sat on the edge of the bandstand and waved the children forward. Kathi and David talked about going. Each would go if the other would. They took napkins for autographs and, holding hands, walked between tables and joined the children standing around Mulligan. When it was their turn he talked to them, signed their napkins, kissed their foreheads. They hurried back to Peter.

"He's *neat*," Kathi said.

"What did you talk about?"

"He asked our names," David said.

"And if we liked winter out here."

"And if we played an instrument."

"What kind of music we liked."

"What did you tell him?"

"Jazz like his."

The second set ended at nearly seven; bourbon-high, Peter drove carefully, listening to Mary Ann and the children talking about Mulligan and his music and warmth. Then David and Kathi were gone, running up the sidewalk to tell Norma, and show their autographed napkins, and Peter followed Mary Ann's directions to her apartment.

"I've been in the same clothes since last night," she said.

In her apartment, as unkempt as his, they showered together, hurried damp-haired and chilled to her bed.

"This is the happiest day I've had since the marriage ended," he said.

But when he went home and was alone in his bed, he saw his cowardice again. All the warmth of his day left him, and he lay in the dark, knowing that he should have been wily enough to understand that the afternoon's sweetness and ease meant he had escaped: had put together a family for the day. That afternoon Kathi had spilled a Coke; before Peter noticed, Mary Ann was cleaning the table with cocktail napkins, smiling at Kathi, talking to her under the music, lifting a hand to the waitress.

Next night he took Mary Ann to dinner and driving to her apartment, it seemed to him that since the end of his marriage, dinner had become disproportionate: alone at home it was a task he forced himself to do, with his children it was a fragile rite, and with old friends who alternately fed him and Norma he felt vaguely criminal. Now he must once again face his failures over a plate of food. He and Mary Ann had slept little the past two nights, and at the restaurant she told him she had worked hard all day, yet she looked fresh and strong, while he was too tired to imagine making love after dinner. With his second martini, he said: "I used you yesterday. With my kids."

"There's a better word."

"All right: needed."

"I knew that."

"You did?"

"We had fun."

"I can't do it anymore."

"Don't be so hard on yourself. You probably spend more time with them now than when you lived together."

"I do. So does Norma. But that's not it. It's how much I wanted your help, and started hoping for it. Next Sunday. And in summer: the sort of stuff you do, camping and hiking; when we talked about it Saturday night—"

"I knew that too. I thought it was sweet."

He leaned back in his chair, sipped his drink. Tonight he would break his martini rule, have a third before dinner. He loved women who knew and forgave his motives before he knew and confessed them.

But he would not take her with the children again. He was with her often; she wanted a lover, she said, not love, not what it still did to men and women. He did not tell her he thought they were using each other in a way that might have been cynical, if it were not so frightening. He simply followed her, became one of those who make love with their friends. But she was his only woman friend, and he did not know how many men shared her. When she told him she would not be home this night or that weekend, he held his questions. He held onto his heart too, and forced himself to make her a part of the times when he was alone. He had married young, and life to him was surrounded by the sounds and touches of a family. Now in this foreign land he felt so vulnerably strange that at times it seemed near madness as he gave Mary Ann a function in his time, ranking somewhere among his running and his work.

When the children asked about her, he said they were still friends. Once Kathi asked why she never came to Lennie's anymore, and he said her work kept her pretty busy and she had other friends she did things with, and he liked being alone with them anyway. But then he was afraid the children thought she had not liked them; so, twice a month, he brought Mary Ann to Lennie's.

He and the children went every Sunday. And that was how the

cold months passed, beginning with the New Year, because Peter and Norma had waited until after Christmas to end the marriage: the movies and sledding, museums and aquarium, the restaurants; always they were on the road, and whenever he looked at his car he thought of the children. How many conversations while looking through the windshield? How many times had the doors slammed shut and they re-entered or left his life? Winter ended slowly. April was cold and in May Peter and the children still wore sweaters or windbreakers, and on two weekends there was rain, and everything they did together was indoors. But when the month ended, Peter thought it was not the weather but the patterns of winter that had kept them driving from place to place.

Then it was June and they were out of school and Peter took his vacation. Norma worked, and by nine in the morning he and Kathi and David were driving to the sea. They took a large blanket and tucked its corners into the sand so it wouldn't flap in the wind, and they lay oiled in the sun. On the first day they talked of winter, how they could feel the sun warming their ribs, as they had watched it warming the earth during the long thaw. It was a beach with gentle currents and a gradual slope out to sea but Peter told them, as he had every summer, about undertow: that if ever they were caught in one, they must not swim against it; they must let it take them out and then they must swim parallel to the beach until the current shifted and they could swim back in with it. He could not imagine his children being calm enough to do that, for he was afraid of water and only enjoyed body-surfing near the beach, but he told them anyway. Then he said it would not happen because he would always test the current first.

In those first two weeks the three of them ran into the water and body-surfed only a few minutes, for it was too cold still, and they had to leave it until their flesh was warm again. They would not be able to stay in long until July. Peter showed them the different colors of summer, told them why on humid days the sky and ocean were paler blue, and on dry days they were darker, more beautiful, and the trees they passed on the roads to the beach were brighter green. He bought a whiffle ball and bat and kept them in the trunk of his car and they played at the beach. The children dug holes, made castles, Peter watched, slept, and in late morning he ran. From a large thermos they drank lemonade or juice; and they ate lunch all day, the children grazing on fruit and the sandwiches he had made before his breakfast. Then he took them to his apartment for showers, and they helped carry in the ice chest and thermos and blanket and their knapsack of clothes. Kathi and David still took turns showering first, and they stayed in longer, but now in summer the water was still hot when his turn came. Then he drove them home to Norma, his skin red and pleasantly burning; then tan.

When his vacation ended they spent all sunny weekends at the sea, and even grey days that were warm. The children became braver about the cold, and forced him to go in with them and bodysurf. But they could stay longer than he could, and he left to lie on the blanket and watch them, to make sure they stayed in shallow water. He made them promise to wait on the beach while he ran. He went in the water to cool his body from the sun, but mostly he lay on the blanket, reading, and watching the children wading out to the breakers and riding them in. Kathi and David did not always stay together. One left to walk the beach alone. Another played with strangers, or children who were there most days too. One built a castle. Another body-surfed. And, often, one would come to the blanket and drink and take a sandwich from the ice chest, would sit eating and drinking beside Peter, offer him a bite, a swallow. And on all those beach days Peter's shyness and apprehension were gone. It's the sea, he said to Mary Ann one night.

And it was: for on that day, a long Saturday at the beach, when he had all day felt peace and father-love and sun and salt water, he had understood why now in summer he and his children were as he had yearned for them to be in winter: they were no longer confined to car or buildings to remind them why they were there. The long beach and the sea were their lawn; the blanket their home; the ice chest and thermos their kitchen. They lived as a family again. While he ran and David dug in the sand until he reached water and Kathi looked for pretty shells for her room, the blanket waited for them. It was the place they wandered back to: for food, for drink, for rest, their talk as casual as between children and father arriving, through separate doors, at the kitchen sink for water, the refrigerator for an orange. Then one left for the surf; another slept in the sun, lips stained with grape juice. He had wanted to tell the children about it, but it was too much to tell, and the beach was no place for such talk anyway, and he also guessed they knew. So that afternoon when they were all lying on the blanket, on their backs, the children flanking him, he simply said: "Divorced kids go to the beach more than married ones."

"Why?" Kathi said.

"Because married people do chores and errands on weekends. No kid-days."

"I love the beach," David said.

"So do I," Peter said.

He looked at Kathi.

"You don't like it, huh?"

She took her arm from her eyes and looked at him. His urge was to turn away. She looked at him for a long time; her eyes were too tender, too wise, and he wished she could have learned both later, and differently; in her eyes he saw the car in winter, heard its doors closing and closing, their talk and the sounds of heater and engine and tires on the road, and the places the car took them. Then she held his hand, and closed her eyes.

"I wish it was summer all year round," she said.

He watched her face, rosy tan now, lightly freckled; her small scar was already lower. Holding her hand, he reached over for David's, and closed his eyes against the sun. His legs touched theirs. After a while he heard them sleeping. Then he slept.

ROSE

In memory of Barbara Loden

Sometimes, when I see people like Rose, I imagine them as babies, as young children. I suppose many of us do. We search the aging skin of the face, the unhappy eyes and mouth. Of course I can never imagine their fat little faces at the breast, or their cheeks flushed and eyes brightened from play. I do not think of them after the age of five or six, when they are sent to kindergartens, to school. There, beyond the shadows of their families and neighborhood friends, they enter the world a second time, their eyes blinking in the light of it. They will be loved or liked or disliked, even hated; some will be ignored, others singled out for daily abuse that, with a few adult exceptions, only children have the energy and heart to inflict. Some will be corrupted, many without knowing it, save for that cooling quiver of conscience when they cheat, when they lie to save themselves, when out of fear they side with bullies or teachers, and so forsake loyalty to a friend. Soon they are small men and women, with our sins and virtues, and by the age of thirteen some have our vices too.

There are also those unforgivable children who never suffer at all: from the first grade on, they are good at schoolwork, at play and sports, and always they are befriended, and are the leaders of the class. Their teachers love them, and because they are humble and warm, their classmates love them too, or at least respect them, and are not envious because they assume these children will excel at whatever they touch, and have long accepted this truth. They come from all manner of families, from poor and illiterate to wealthy and what passes for literate in America, and no one knows why they are not only athletic and attractive but intelligent too. This is an injustice, and some of us pause for a few moments in our middle-aged lives to remember the pain of childhood, and then we intensely dislike these people we applauded and courted, and we hope some crack of mediocrity we could not see with our young eyes has widened and split open their lives, the homecoming queen's radiance sallowed by tranquilized bitterness, the quarterback fat at forty wheezing up a flight of stairs, and all of them living in the same small town or city neighborhood, laboring at vacuous work that turns their memories to those halcyon days when the classrooms and halls, the playgrounds and gymnasiums and dance floors were theirs: the last places that so obediently, even lovingly, welcomed the weight of their flesh, and its displacement of air. Then, with a smile, we rid ourselves of that evil wish, let it pass from our bodies to dissipate like smoke in the air around us, and, freed from the distraction of blaming some classmate's excellence for our childhood pain, we focus on the boy or girl we were, the small body we occupied, watch it growing through the summers and school years, and we see that, save for some strengths gained here, some weaknesses there, we are the same people we first knew as ourselves; or the ones memory allows us to see, to think we know.

People like Rose make me imagine them in those few years their memories will never disclose, except through hearsay: *I was born in Austin. We lived in a garage apartment. When I was two we moved to Tuscaloosa. . . .* Sometimes, when she is drinking at the bar, and I am standing some distance from her and can watch without her noticing, I see her as a baby, on the second or third floor of a tenement, in one of the Massachusetts towns along the Merrimack River. She would not notice, even if she turned and looked at my face; she would know me, she would speak to me, but she would not know I had been watching. Her face, sober or drunk or on the way to it, looks constantly watched, even spoken to, by her own soul. Or by something it has spawned, something that lives always with her, hovering near her face. I see her in a tenement because I cannot imagine her coming from any but a poor family, though I sense this notion comes from my boyhood, from something I learned about America, and that belief has hardened inside me, a stone I cannot dissolve. Snobbishness is too simple a word for it. I have never had much money. Nor do I want it. No: it's an old belief, once a philosophy, which I've now outgrown: no one born to a white family with adequate money could end as Rose has.

I know it's not true. I am fifty-one years old, yet I cannot feel I am growing older because I keep repeating the awakening experiences of a child: I watch and I listen, I write in my journal, and each year I discover, with the awe of my boyhood, a part of the human spirit I had perhaps imagined, but had never seen or heard. When I was a boy, many of these discoveries thrilled me. Once in school the teacher told us of the men who volunteered to help find the cause of yellow fever. This was in the Panama Canal Zone. Some of these men lived in the room where victims of yellow fever had died; they lay on the beds, on sheets with dried black vomit, breathed and slept there. Others sat in a room with mosquitoes and gave their skin to those bites we simply curse and slap, and they waited through the itching and more bites, and then waited to die, in their agony leaving sheets like the ones that spared their comrades living in the room of the dead. This story, with its heroism, its infinite possibilities for human action, delighted me with the pure music of hope. I am afraid now to research it, for I may find that the men were convicts awaiting execution, or some other persons whose lives were so limited by stronger outside forces that the risk of death to save others could not have, for them, the clarity of a choice made with courage, and in sacrifice, but could be only a weary nod of assent to yet another fated occurrence in their lives. But their story cheered me then, and I shall cling to that. Don't you remember? When first you saw or heard or read about men and women who, in the face of some defiant circumstance, fought against themselves and won, and so achieved love, honor, courage?

I was in the Marine Corps for three years, a lieutenant during a time in our country when there was no war but all the healthy young men had to serve in the armed forces anyway. Many of us who went to college sought commissions so our service would be easier, we would have more money, and we could marry our girlfriends; in those days, a young man had to provide a roof and all that goes under it before he could make love with his girl. Of course there was love-making in cars, but the ring and the roof waited somewhere beyond the windshield.

Those of us who chose the Marines went to Quantico, Virginia, for two six-week training sessions in separate summers during college; we were commissioned at graduation from college, and went back to Quantico, for eight months of Officers' Basic School; only then would they set us free among the troops, and into the wise care of our platoon sergeants. During the summer training, which was called Platoon Leaders' Class, sergeants led us, harrassed us, and taught us. They also tried to make some of us quit. I'm certain that when they first lined us up and looked at us, their professional eyes saw the ones who would not complete the course: saw in a young boy's stiffened shoulders and staring and blinking eyes the flaw—too much fear, lack of confidence, who knows—that would, in a few weeks, possess him. Just as, on the first day of school, the bully sees his victim and eyes him like a cat whose prey has wandered too far from safety; it is not the boy's puny body that draws the bully, but the way the boy's spirit occupies his small chest, his thin arms.

Soon the sergeants left alone the stronger among us, and focused their energy on breaking the ones they believed would break, and ought to break now, rather than later, in that future war they probably did not want but never forgot. In another platoon, that first summer, a boy from Dartmouth completed the course, though in six weeks his crew-cut black hair turned gray. The boy in our platoon was from the University of Chicago, and he should not have come to Quantico. He was physically weak. The sergeants liked the smaller ones among us, those with short lean bodies. They called them feather merchants, told them You little guys are always tough, and issued them the Browning Automatic Rifle for marches and field exercises, because it weighed twenty pounds and had a cumbersome bulk to it as well: there was no way you could comfortably carry it. But the boy from Chicago was short and thin and weak, and they despised him.

Our platoon sergeant was a staff sergeant, his assistant a buck sergeant, and from the first day they worked on making the boy quit. We all knew he would fail the course; we waited only to see whether he would quit and go home before they sent him. He did not quit. He endured five weeks before the company commander summoned him to his office. He was not there long; he came into the squad bay where he lived and changed to civilian clothes, packed the suitcase and seabag, and was gone. In those five weeks he had dropped out of conditioning marches, forcing himself up hills in the Virginia heat, carrying seventy pounds of gear—probably half his weight—until he collapsed on the trail to the sound of shouted derision from our sergeants, whom I doubt he heard.

When he came to Quantico he could not chin himself, nor do ten push-ups. By the time he left he could chin himself five quivering times, his back and shoulders jerking, and he could do twenty push-ups before his shoulders and chest rose while his small flat belly stayed on the ground. I do not remember his name, but I remember those numbers: five and twenty. The sergeants humiliated him daily, gave him long and colorful ass-chewings, but their true weapon was his own body, and they put it to use. They ran him till he fell, then ran him again, a sergeant running alongside the boy, around and around the hot blacktop parade ground. They sent him up and down the rope on the obstacle course. He never climbed it, but they sent him as far up as he could go, perhaps halfway, perhaps less, and when

he froze, then worked his way down, they sent him up again. That's
the phrase: *as far up as he could go.*

He should not have come to Virginia. What was he thinking?
Why didn't he get himself in shape during the school year, while he
waited in Chicago for what he must have known would be the physical trial of his life? I understand now why the sergeants despised him,
this weak college boy who wanted to be one of their officers. Most
nights they went out drinking, and once or twice a week came into
our squad bay, drunk at three in the morning, to turn on the lights
and shout us out of our bunks, and we stood at attention and listened
to their cheerful abuse. Three hours later, when we fell out for morning chow, they waited for us: lean and tanned and immaculate in their
tailored and starched dungarees and spit-shined boots. And the boy
could only go so far up the rope, up the series of hills we climbed, up
toward the chinning bar, up the walls and angled poles of the obstacle course, up from the grass by the strength of his arms as the rest of
us reached fifty, seventy, finally a hundred push-ups.

But in truth he could do all of it, and that is the reason for this
anecdote while I contemplate Rose. One night in our fifth week the
boy walked in his sleep. Every night we had fire watch: one of us
walked for four hours through the barracks, the three squad bays that
each housed a platoon, to alert the rest in case of fire. We heard the
story next day, whispered, muttered, or spoken out of the boy's hearing, in the chow hall, during the ten-minute break on a march. The
fire watch was a boy from the University of Alabama, a football
player whose southern accent enriched his story, heightened his surprise, his awe. He came into our squad bay at three-thirty in the
morning, looked up and down the rows of bunks, and was about to
leave when he heard someone speak. The voice frightened him. He
had never heard, except in movies, a voice so pitched by desperation,
and so eerie in its insistence. He moved toward it. Behind our bunks,
against both walls, were our wall lockers. The voice came from that
space between the bunks and lockers, where there was room to stand
and dress, and to prepare your locker for inspection. The Alabama

boy stepped between the bunks and lockers and moved toward the figure he saw now: someone squatted before a locker, white shorts and white tee shirt in the darkness. Then he heard what the voice was saying. *I can't find it. I can't find it.* He closed the distance between them, squatted, touched the boy's shoulder, and whispered: *Hey, what you looking for?* Then he saw it was the boy from Chicago. He spoke his name, but the boy bent lower and looked under his wall locker. That was when the Alabama boy saw that he was not truly looking: his eyes were shut, the lids in the repose of sleep, while the boy's head shook from side to side, in a short slow arc of exasperation. *I can't find it,* he said. He was kneeling before the wall locker, bending forward to look under it for—what? any of the several small things the sergeant demanded we care for and have with our gear: extra shoelaces, a web strap from a haversack, a metal button for dungarees, any of these things that became for us as precious as talismans. Still on his knees, the boy straightened his back, gripped the bottom of the wall locker, and lifted it from the floor, six inches or more above it, and held it there as he tried to lower his head to look under it. The locker was steel, perhaps six feet tall, and filled with his clothes, boots, and shoes, and on its top rested his packed haversack and helmet. No one in the platoon could have lifted it while kneeling, using only his arms. Most of us could have bear-hugged it up from the floor, even held it there. *Gawd damn,* the fire watch said, rising from his squat; *Gawd damn, lemmee help you with it,* and he held its sides; it was tottering, but still raised. Gently he lowered it against the boy's resistance, then crouched again and, whispering to him, *like to a baby,* he told us, he said: *All rot, now. It'll be all rot now. We'll fin' that damn thing in the mawnin';* as he tried to ease the boy's fingers from the bottom edge of the locker. Finally he pried them, one or two at a time. He pulled the boy to his feet, and with an arm around his waist, led him to his bunk. It was a lower bunk. He eased the boy downward to sit on it, then lifted his legs, covered him with the sheet, and sat down beside him. He rested a hand on the boy's chest, and spoke soothingly to him as he struggled, trying to rise.

Finally the boy lay still, his hands holding the top of the sheet near his chest.

We never told him. He went home believing his body had failed; he was the only failure in our platoon, and the only one in the company who failed because he lacked physical strength and endurance. I've often wondered about him: did he ever learn what he could truly do? Has he ever absolved himself of his failure? His was another of the inspiring stories of my youth. Not *his* story so much as the story of his body. I had heard or read much about the human spirit, indomitable against suffering and death. But this was a story of a pair of thin arms, and narrow shoulders, and weak legs: freed from whatever consciousness did to them, they had lifted an unwieldy weight they could not have moved while the boy's mind was awake. It is a mystery I still do not understand.

Now, more often than not, my discoveries are bad ones, and if they inspire me at all, it is only to try to understand the unhappiness and often evil in the way we live. A friend of mine, a doctor, told me never again to believe that only the poor and uneducated and usually drunk beat their children; or parents who are insane, who hear voices commanding them to their cruelty. He has seen children, sons and daughters of doctors, bruised, their small bones broken, and he knows that the children are repeating their parents' lies: they fell down the stairs, they slipped and struck a table. He can do nothing for them but heal their injuries. The poor are frightened by authority, he said, and they will open their doors to a social worker. A doctor will not. And I have heard stories from young people, college students who come to the bar during the school year. They are rich, or their parents are, and they have about them those characteristics I associate with the rich: they look healthy, as though the power of money had a genetic influence on their very flesh; beneath their laughter and constant talk there lies always a certain poise, not sophistication, but confidence in life and their places in it. Perhaps it comes from the knowledge that they will never be stranded in a bus station with two dollars. But probably its source is more intangible: the ambience they grew up in: that strange paradox of being from birth removed, insulated, from most of the world, and its agony of survival that is, for most of us, a day-to-day life; while, at the same time, these young rich children are exposed, through travel and—some of them—culture, to more of the world than most of us will ever see.

Years ago, when the students first found Timmy's and made it their regular drinking place, I did not like them, because their lives were so distant from those of the working men who patronize the bar. Then some of them started talking to me, in pairs, or a lone boy or girl, drinking near my spot at the bar's corner. I began enjoying their warmth, their general cheer, and often I bought them drinks, and always they bought mine in return. They called me by my first name, and each new class knows me, as they know Timmy's, before they see either of us. When they were alone, or with a close friend, they talked to me about themselves, revealed beneath that underlying poise deep confusion, and abiding pain their faces belied. So I learned of the cruelties of some of the rich: of children beaten, girls fondled by fathers who were never drunk and certainly did not smoke, healthy men who were either crazy or evil beneath their suits and briefcases, and their punctuality and calm confidence that crossed the line into arrogance. I learned of neglect: children reared by live-in nurses, by housekeepers who cooked; children in summer camps and boarding schools; and I saw the selfishness that wealth allows, a selfishness beyond greed, a desire to have children yet give them nothing, or very little, of oneself. I know one boy, an only child, whose mother left home when he was ten. She no longer wanted to be a mother; she entered the world of business in a city across the country from him, and he saw her for a weekend once a year. His father worked hard at making more money, and the boy left notes on the door of his father's den, asking for a time to see him. An appointment. The father answered with notes on the boy's door, and they met. Then the boy came to college here. He is very serious, very polite, and I have never seen him with a girl, or another boy, and I have never seen him smile.

So I have no reason to imagine Rose on that old stained carpet with places of it worn thin, nearly to the floor; Rose crawling among the legs of older sisters and brothers, looking up at the great and burdened height of her parents, their capacity, their will to love long beaten or drained from them by what they had to do to keep a dwelling with food in it, and heat in it, and warm and cool clothes for their children. I have only guessed at this part of her history. There is one reason, though: Rose's face is bereft of education, of thought. It is the face of a survivor walking away from a terrible car accident: without memory or conjecture, only shock, and the surprise of knowing that she is indeed alive. I think of her body as shapeless: beneath the large and sagging curve of her breasts, she has such sparse curvature of hips and waist that she appears to be an elongated lump beneath her loose dresses in summer, her old wool overcoat in winter. At the bar she does not remove her coat; but she unbuttons it and pushes it back from her breasts, and takes the blue scarf from her head, shakes her graying brown hair, and lets the scarf hang from her neck.

She appeared in our town last summer. We saw her on the streets, or slowly walking across the bridge over the Merrimack River. Then she found Timmy's and, with money from whatever source, became a regular, along with the rest of us. Sometimes, if someone drank beside her, she spoke. If no one drank next to her, she drank alone. Always screwdrivers. Then we started talking about her and, with that ear for news that impresses me still about small communities, either towns or city neighborhoods, some of us told stories about her. Rumors: she had been in prison, or her husband, or someone else in the family had. She had children but lost them. Someone had heard of a murder: perhaps she killed her husband, or one of the children did, or he or Rose or both killed a child. There was talk of a fire. And so we talked for months, into the fall, then early winter, when our leaves are gone, the reds and golds and yellows, and the trees are bare and gray, the evergreens dark green, and beyond their conical green we have lovely early sunsets. When the sky is gray, the earth is washed with it, and the evergreens look black. Then the ponds freeze and snow comes silently one night, and we wake to a white earth. It was during an early snowstorm when one of us said that Rose worked in a leather factory in town, had been there since she had appeared last summer. He knew someone who worked there and saw her. He knew nothing else.

On a night in January, while a light and pleasant snow dusted the tops of cars, and the shoulders and hats and scarves of people coming into Timmy's, Rose told me her story. I do not know whether, afterward, she was glad or relieved; neither of us has mentioned it since. Nor have our eyes, as we greet each other, sometimes chat. And one night I was without money, or enough of it, and she said *I owe you*, and bought the drinks. But that night in January she was in the state when people finally must talk. She was drunk too, or close enough to it, but I know her need to talk was there before vodka released her. I won't try to record our conversation. It was interrupted by one or both of us going to the bathroom, or ordering drinks (I insisted on paying for them all, and after the third round she simply thanked me, and patted my hand); interrupted by people leaning between us for drinks to bring back to booths, by people who came to speak to me, happy people oblivious of Rose, men or women or students who stepped to my side and began talking with that alcoholic lack of manners or awareness of intruding that, in a neighborhood bar, is not impolite but a part of the fabric of conversation. Interrupted too by the radio behind the bar, the speakers at both ends of the room, the loud rock music from an FM station in Boston.

It was a Friday, so the bar closed at two instead of one; we started talking at eleven. Gradually, before that, Rose had pushed her way down the bar toward my corner. I had watched her move to the right to make room for a couple, again to allow a man to squeeze in beside her, and again for some college girls; then the two men to my left went home, and when someone else wedged his arms and shoulders between the standing drinkers at the bar, she stepped to her right again and we faced each other across the corner. We talked about the bartender (we liked him), the crowd (we liked them: loud, but generally peaceful) and she said she always felt safe at Timmy's because everybody knew everybody else, and they didn't allow trouble in here.

"I can't stand fighting bars," she said. "Those young punks that have to hit somebody."

We talked about the weather, the seasons. She liked fall. The factory was too hot in summer. So was her apartment. She had bought a large fan, and it was so loud you could hear it from outside, and it blew dust from the floor, ashes from ashtrays. She liked winter, the snow, and the way the cold made her feel more alive; but she was afraid of it too: she was getting old, and did not want to be one of those people who slipped on ice and broke a hip.

"The old bones," she said. "They don't mend like young ones."

"You're no older than I am."

"Oh yes I am. And you'd better watch your step too. On that ice," and she nodded at the large front window behind me.

"That's snow," I said. "A light, dry snow."

She smiled at me, her face affectionate, and coquettish with some shared secret, as though we were talking in symbols. Then she finished her drink and I tried to get Steve's attention. He is a large man, and was mixing drinks at the other end of the bar. He did not look our way, so finally I called his name, my voice loud enough to be heard, but softened with courtesy to a tenor. Off and on, through the years, I have tended bar, and I am sensitive about the matter of ordering from a bartender who is making several drinks and, from the people directly in front of him, hearing requests for more. He heard me and glanced at us and I raised two fingers; he nodded. When I looked at Rose again she was gazing down into her glass, as though studying the yellow-filmed ice.

"I worry about fires in winter," she said, still looking down. "Sometimes every night."

"When you're going to sleep? You worry about a fire?"

She looked at me.

"Nearly every night."

"What kind of heat does your building have?"

"Oil furnace."

"Is something wrong with it?"

"No."

"Then—" Steve is very fast; he put my beer and her screwdriver before us, and I paid him; he spun, strode to the cash register, jabbed it, slapped in my ten, and was back with the change. I pushed a dollar toward him, and he thanked me and was gone, repeating an order from the other end of the bar, and a rock group sang above the crowd, a ceiling of sound over the shouts, the laughter, and the crescendo of juxtaposed conversations.

"Then why are you worried?" I said. "Were you in a fire? As a child?"

"I was. Not in winter. And I sure wasn't no child. But you hear them. The sirens. All the time in winter."

"Wood stoves," I said. "Faulty chimneys."

"They remind me. The sirens. Sometimes it isn't even the sirens. I try not to think about them. But sometimes it's like they think about me. They do. You know what I mean?"

"The sirens?"

"*No.*" She grabbed my wrist and squeezed it, hard as a man might; I had not known the strength of her hands. "The flames," she said.

"The flames?"

"I'm not doing anything. Or I'm at work, packing boxes. With leather. Or I'm going to sleep. Or right now, just then, we were talking about winter. I try not to think about them. But here they come, and I can see them. I feel them. Little flames. Big ones. Then—"

She released my wrist, swallowed from her glass, and her face changed: a quick recognition of something forgotten. She patted my hand.

"Thanks for the drink."

"I have money tonight."

"Good. Some night you won't, and I will. You'll drink on me."

"Fine."

"Unless you slip on that ice," nodding her head toward the window, the gentle snow, her eyes brightening again with that shared mystery, their luster near anger, not at me but at what we shared.

"Then what?" I said.

"What?"

"When you see them. When you feel the fire."

"My kids."

"No."

"Three kids."

"No, Rose."

"Two were upstairs. We lived on the third floor."

"Please: no stories like that tonight."

She patted my hand, as though in thanks for a drink, and said: "Did you lose a child?"

"Yes."

"In a fire?"

"A car."

"You poor man. Don't cry."

And with her tough thumbs she wiped the beginning of my tears from beneath my eyes, then standing on tiptoe she kissed my cheek, her lips dry, her cheek as it brushed mine feeling no softer than my own, save for her absence of whiskers.

"Mine got out," she said. "I got them out."

I breathed deeply and swallowed beer and wiped my eyes, but she had dried them.

"And it's the only thing I ever did. In my whole fucking life. The only thing I ever did that was worth a shit."

"Come on. Nobody's like that."

"No?"

"I hope nobody is."

I looked at the clock on the opposite wall; it was near the speaker that tilted downward, like those mirrors in stores, so cashiers can watch people between shelves. From the speaker came a loud electric guitar, repeating a series of chords, then two or more frenetic saxophones blowing their hoarse tones at the heads of the drinkers, like an indoor storm without rain. On that clock the time was two minutes till midnight, so I knew it was eleven thirty-eight; at Timmy's they keep the clock twenty minutes fast. This allows them time to give last call and still get the patrons out by closing. Rose was talking. Sometimes I watched her; sometimes I looked away, when I could do that and still hear. For when I listened while watching faces I knew, hearing some of their voices, I did not see everything she told me: I saw, but my vision was dulled, given distance, by watching bearded Steve work, or the blond student Ande laughing over the mouth of her beer bottle, or old gray-haired Lou, retired from his job as a factory foreman, drinking his shots and drafts, and smoking Camels; or the young owner Timmy, in his mid-thirties, wearing a leather jacket and leaning on the far corner of the bar, drinking club soda and watching the hockey game that was silent under the sounds of rock.

But most of the time, because of the noise, I had to look at her eyes or mouth to hear; and when I did that, I saw everything, without the distractions of sounds and faces and bodies, nor even the softening of distance, of time: I saw the two little girls, and the little boy, their pallid terrified faces; I saw their father's big arm and hand arcing down in a slap; in a blow with his fist closed; I saw the five-year-old boy, the oldest, flung through the air, across the room, to strike the wall and drop screaming to the couch against it. Toward the end, nearly his only sounds were screams; he virtually stopped talking, and lived as a frightened yet recalcitrant prisoner. And in Rose's eyes I saw the embers of death, as if the dying of her spirit had come not with a final yielding sigh, but in a blaze of recognition.

It was long ago, in a Massachusetts town on the Merrimack River. Her husband was a big man, with strongly muscled arms, and the solid rounded belly of a man who drinks much beer at night and works hard, with his body, five days a week. He was handsome, too. His face was always reddish-brown from his outdoor work, his hair was thick and black, and curls of it topped his forehead, and when he wore his cap on the back of his head, the visor rested on his curls. He had a thick but narrow mustache, and on Friday and Saturday nights, when they went out to drink and dance, he dressed in brightly colored pants and shirts that his legs and torso and arms filled. His name was Jim Cormier, his grandfather Jacques had come from Quebec as a young man, and his father was Jacques Cormier too, and by Jim's generation the last name was pronounced *Cormeer*, and he was James. Jim was a construction worker, but his physical strength and endurance were unequally complemented by his mind, his spirit, whatever that element is that draws the attention of other men. He was best at the simplest work, and would never be a foreman, or tradesman. Other men, when he worked with them, baffled him. He did not have the touch: could not be entrusted to delegate work, to plan, to oversee, and to handle men. Bricks and mortar and trowels and chalk lines baffled him too, as did planes and levels; yet when he drank at home every night—they seldom went out after the children were born—he talked about learning to operate heavy equipment.

Rose did not tell me all this at first. She told me the end, the final night, and only in the last forty minutes or so, when I questioned her, did she go further back, to the beginning. Where I start her story, so I can try to understand how two young people married, with the hope of love—even, in those days before pandemic divorce, the certainty of love—and within six years, when they were still young, still in their twenties, their home had become a horror for their children, for Rose, and yes: for Jim. A place where a boy of five, and girls of four and three, woke, lived, and slept in isolation from the light of a child's life: the curiosity, the questions about birds, appliances, squirrels and trees and snow and rain, and the first heart-quickening of love for another child, not a sister or brother, but the boy or girl in a sandbox or on a tricycle at the house down the street. They lived always in darkness, deprived even of childhood fears of ghosts in the shadowed corners of the rooms where they slept, deprived of dreams of vicious and carnivorous monsters. Their young memories and

their present consciousness were the tall broad man and his redden-
ing face that shouted and hissed, and his large hands. Rose must have
had no place at all, or very little, in their dreams and in their wary
and apprehensive minds when they were awake. Unless as a wish: I
imagine them in their beds, in the moments before sleep, hoping for
Rose to take them in her arms, carry them one by one to the car
while the giant slept drunkenly in the bed she shared with him, Rose
putting their toys and clothes in the car's trunk, and driving with
them far away to a place—what place could they imagine? What
place not circumscribed by their apartment's walls, whose very colors and hanging pictures and calendar were for them the dark gray
of fear and pain? Certainly, too, in those moments before sleep, they
must have wished their father gone. Simply gone. The boy may have
thought of, wished for, Jim's death. The younger girls, four and
three, only that he vanish, leaving no trace of himself in their home,
in their hearts, not even guilt. Simply vanish.

Rose was a silent partner. If there is damnation, and a place for the
damned, it must be a quiet place, where spirits turn away from each
other and stand in solitude and gaze haplessly at eternity. For it must
be crowded with the passive: those people whose presence in life was
a paradox; for, while occupying space and moving through it and
making sounds in it they were obviously present, while in truth they
were not: they witnessed evil and lifted neither an arm nor voice to
stop it, they witnessed joy and neither sang nor clapped their hands.
But so often we understand them too easily, tolerate them too much:
they have universality, so we forgive the man who watches injustice,
a drowning, a murder, because he reminds us of ourselves, and we
share with him the loyal bond of cowardice, whether once or a hundred times we have turned away from another's suffering to save ourselves: our jobs, our public selves, our bones and flesh. And these
people are so easy to pity. We know fear as early as we know love,
and fear is always with us. I have friends my own age who still cannot say what they believe, except in the most intimate company.

Condemning the actively evil man is a simple matter, though we tend not only to forgive but cheer him if he robs banks or Brink's, and outwits authority: those unfortunate policemen, minions whose uniforms and badges and revolvers are, for many of us, a distorted symbol of what we fear: not a fascist state but a Power, a God, who knows all our truths, believes none of our lies, and with that absolute knowledge will both judge and exact punishment. For we see to it that no one absolutely knows us, so at times the passing blue figure of a policeman walking his beat can stir in us our fear of discovery. We like to see them made into dupes by the outlaw.

But if the outlaw rapes, tortures, gratuitously kills, or if he makes children suffer, we hate him with a purity we seldom feel: our hatred has no roots in prejudice, or self-righteousness, but in horror. He has done something we would never do, something we could not do even if we wished it; our bodies would not obey, would not tear the dress, or lift and swing the axe, pull the trigger, throw the screaming child across the room. So I hate Jim Cormier, and cannot understand him; cannot with my imagination cross the distance between myself and him, enter his soul and know how it felt to live even five minutes of his life. And I forgive Rose, but as I write I resist that compassion, or perhaps merely empathy, and force myself to think instead of the three children, and Rose living there, knowing what she knew. She was young.

She is Irish: a Callahan till marriage, and she and Jim were Catholic. Devout Catholics, she told me. By that, she did not mean they strived to live in imitation of Christ. She meant they did not practice artificial birth control, but rhythm, and after their third year of marriage they had three children. They left the Church then. That is, they stopped attending Sunday Mass and receiving Communion. Do you see? I am not a Catholic, but even I know that they were never truly members of that faith, and so could not have left it. There is too much history, too much philosophy involved, for the matter of faith to rest finally and solely on the use of contraceptives. That was long ago, and now my Catholic friends tell me the priests no longer concern themselves with birth control. But we must live in our own time; Thomas More died for an issue that would have no meaning today. Rose and Jim, though, were not Thomas Mores. They could not see a single act as a renunciation or affirmation of a belief, a way of life. No. They had neither a religion nor a philosophy; like most people I know, their philosophies were simply their accumulated reactions to their daily circumstance, their lives as they lived them from one hour to the next. They were not driven, guided, by either passionate belief or strong resolve. And for that I pity them both, as I pity the others who move through life like scraps of paper in the wind.

With contraception they had what they believed were two years of freedom. There had been a time when all three of their children wore diapers, and only the boy could walk, and with him holding her coat or pants, moving so slowly beside her, Rose went daily to the laundromat, pushing two strollers, gripping a paper grocery bag of soiled diapers, with a clean bag folded in her purse. Clorox rested underneath one stroller, a box of soap underneath the other. While she waited for the diapers to wash, the boy walked among the machines, touched them, watched them, and watched the other women who waited. The oldest girl crawled about on the floor. The baby slept in Rose's lap, or nursed in those days when mothers did not expose their breasts, and Rose covered the infant's head, and her breast, with her unbuttoned shirt. The children became hungry, or tired, or restless, and they fussed, and cried, as Rose called to the boy to leave the woman alone, to stop playing with the ashtray, the soap, and she put the diapers in the dryer. And each day she felt that the other women, even those with babies, with crawling and barely walking children, with two or three children, and one pregnant with a third, had about them some grace, some calm, that kept their voices soft, their gestures tender; she watched them with shame, and a deep dislike of herself, but no envy, as if she had tried out for a dance company and on the first day had entered a room of slender professionals in leotards, dancing like cats, while she clumsily moved her heavy body clad in gray sweatclothes. Most of the time she changed the diaper of at least one of the children, and dropped it in the bag, the beginning of tomorrow's load. If the baby slept in her stroller, and the older girl and the boy played on the floor, Rose folded the diapers on the table in the laundromat, talking and smoking with the other women. But that was rare: the chance that all three small children could at the same time be peaceful and without need, and so give her peace. Imagine: three of them with bladders and bowels, thirst, hunger, fatigue, and none of them synchronized. Most days she put the hot unfolded diapers in the clean bag and hurried home.

Finally she cried at dinner one night for a washing machine and a dryer, and Jim stared at her, not with anger, or impatience, and not refusal either: but with the resigned look of a man who knew he could neither refuse it nor pay for it. It was the washing machine; he would buy it with monthly payments, and when he had done that, he would get the dryer. He sank posts in the earth and nailed boards across their tops and stretched clotheslines between them. He said in rain or freezing cold she would have to hang the wet diapers over the backs of chairs. It was all he could do. Until he could get her a dryer. And when he came home on those days of rain or cold, he looked surprised, as if rain and cold in New England were as foreign to him as the diapers that seemed to occupy the house. He removed them from the rod for the shower curtain, and when he had cleaned his work from his body, he hung them again. He took them from the arms and back of his chair and laid them on top of others, on a chair, or the edges of the kitchen table. Then he sat in the chair whose purpose he had restored; he drank beer and gazed at the drying diapers, as if they were not cotton at all, but the whitest of white shades of the dead, come to haunt him, to assault him, an inch at a time, a foot, until they won, surrounded him where he stood in some corner of the bedroom, the bathroom, in the last place in his home that was his. His *quercençia*: his cool or blood-smelling sand, the only spot in the bull-ring where he wanted to stand and defend, to lower his head and wait.

He struck the boy first, before contraception and the freedom and new life it promised, as money does. Rose was in the kitchen, chopping onions, now and then turning her face to wipe, with the back of her wrist, the tears from her eyes. The younger girl was asleep; the older one crawled between and around Rose's legs. The boy was three. She had nearly finished the onions and could put them in the skillet and stop crying, when she heard the slap, and knew what it was in that instant before the boy cried: a different cry: in it she heard not only startled fear, but a new sound: a wail of betrayal, of pain from the heart. Wiping her hands on her apron, she went quickly to the living room, into that long and loudening cry, as if the boy, with each moment of deeper recognition, raised his voice until it howled. He stood in front of his seated father. Before she reached him, he looked at her, as though without hearing footsteps or seeing her from the corner of his blurred wet vision, he knew she was there. She was his mother. Yet when he turned his face to her, it was not with appeal: above his small reddened cheeks he looked into her eyes; and in his, as tears ran from them, was that look whose sound she had heard in the kitchen. Betrayal. Accusing her of it, and without anger, only with dismay. In her heart she felt something fall between herself and her son, like a glass wall, or a space that spanned only a few paces, yet was infinite, and she could never cross it again. Now his voice had attained the howl, and though his cheeks were wet, his eyes were dry now; or anyway tearless, for they looked wet and bright as pools that could reflect her face. The baby was awake, crying in her crib. Rose looked from her son's eyes to her husband's. They were dark, and simpler than the boy's: in them she saw only the ebb of his fury: anger, and a resolve to preserve and defend it.

"I told him not to," he said.

"Not to what?"

"Climb on my legs. Look." He pointed to a dark wet spot on the carpet. "He spilled the beer."

She stared at the spot. She could not take her eyes from it. The baby was crying, and the muscles of her legs tried to move toward that sound. Then she realized her son was silent. She felt him watching her, and she would not look at him.

"It's nothing to cry about," Jim said.

"You *slapped* him."

"Not *him*. You."

"Me? That's onions."

She wiped her hands on her apron, brushed her eyes with the back of her wrist.

"Jesus," she said. She looked at her son. She had to look away from those eyes. Then she saw the older girl: she had come to the doorway, and was standing on the threshold, her thumb in her mouth; above her small closed fist and nose, her frightened eyes stared, and she looked as though she were trying not to cry. But, if she was, there could be only one reason for a child so young: she was afraid for her voice to leave her, to enter the room, where now Rose could feel her children's fear as tangibly as a cold draft blown through a cracked windowpane. Her legs, her hips, strained toward the baby's cry for food, a dry diaper, for whatever acts of love they need when they wake, and even more when they wake before they are ready, when screams smash the shell of their sleep. "Jesus," she said, and hurried out of the room where the pain in her son's heart had pierced her own, and her little girl's fearful silence pierced it again; or slashed it, for she felt as she bent over the crib that she was no longer whole, that her height and breadth and depth were in pieces that somehow held together, did not separate and drop to the floor, through it, into the earth itself.

"I should have hit him with the skillet," she said to me, so many years later, after she had told me the end and I had drawn from her the beginning, in the last half-hour of talk.

She could not hit him that night. With the heavy iron skillet, with its hot oil waiting for the onions. For by then something had flowed away from Rose, something of her spirit simply wafting willy-nilly out of her body, out of the apartment, and it never came back, not even with the diaphragm. Perhaps it began to leave her at the laundromat, or in bed at night, at the long day's end not too tired for lust, for rutting, but too tired for an evening of desire that began with dinner and crested and fell and crested again through the hours as they lay close and naked in bed, from early in the night until finally they slept. On the car seat of courtship she had dreamed of this, and in the first year of marriage she lived the dream: joined him in the shower and made love with him, still damp, before they went to the dinner kept warm on the stove, then back to the bed's tossed sheets to lie in the dark, smoking, talking, touching, and they made love again; and, later, again, until they could only lie side by side waiting for their breathing to slow, before they slept. Now at the tired ends of days they took release from each other, and she anxiously slept, waiting for a baby to cry.

Or perhaps it left her between the shelves of a supermarket. His payday was Thursday, and by then the refrigerator and cupboard were nearly empty. She shopped on Friday. Unless a neighbor could watch the children, Rose shopped at night, when Jim was home; they ate early and she hurried to the store to shop before it closed. Later, months after he slapped the boy, she believed his rage had started then, alone in the house with them, changing the baby and putting her in the crib while the other girl and the boy spat and flung food from their highchairs where she had left them, in her race with time to fill a cart with food Jim could afford: she looked at the price of everything she took from a shelf. She did not believe, later, that he struck them on those nights. But there must have been rage, the frightening voice of it; for he was tired, and confused, and over-whelmed by three small people with wills of their own, and no control over the needs of their bodies and their spirits. Certainly he must have yelled; maybe he squeezed an arm, or slapped a rump. When she returned with the groceries, the apartment was quiet: the children slept, and he sat in the kitchen, with the light out, drinking beer. A light from the living room behind him and around a corner showed her his silhouette: large and silent, a cigarette glowing at his mouth, a beer bottle rising to it. Then he would turn on the light and put down his beer and walk past her, to the old car, to carry in the rest of the groceries.

When finally two of the children could walk, Rose went to the supermarket during the day, the boy and girl walking beside her, behind her, away from her voice whose desperate pitch embarrassed her, as though its sound were a sign to the other women with children that she was incompetent, unworthy to be numbered among them. The boy and girl took from shelves cookies, crackers, cereal boxes, cans of vegetables and fruit, sometimes to play with them, but at other times to bring to her, where holding the cart they pulled themselves up on the balls of their feet and dropped in the box, or the can. Still she scolded them, jerked the can or box from the cart, brought it back to its proper place; and when she did this, her heart sank as though pulled by a sigh deeper into her body. For she saw. She saw that when the children played with these things whose colors or shapes drew them so they wanted to sit on the floor and hold or turn in their hands the box or can, they were simply being children whom she could patiently teach, if patience were still an element in her spirit. And that when they brought things to her, to put into the cart, repeating the motions of their mother, they were joining, without fully knowing it, the struggle of the family, and without knowing the struggle that was their parents' lives. Their hearts, though, must have expected praise; or at least an affectionate voice, a gentle hand, to show that their mother did not need what they had brought her. If only there were time: one extra hour of grocery shopping to spend in this gentle instruction. Or if she had strength to steal the hour anyway, despite the wet and tired and staring baby in the cart. But she could not: she scolded, she jerked from the cart or their hands the things they had brought, and the boy became quiet, the girl sucked her thumb and held Rose's pants as the four of them moved with the cart between the long shelves. The baby fussed, with that unceasing low cry that was not truly crying, only wordless sounds of fatigue. Rose recognized it, understood it, for by now she had learned the awful lesson of fatigue, which as a young girl she had never felt. She knew that it was worse than the flu, whose enforced rest at least left you the capacity to care for someone else, to mutter words of love; but that, healthy, you could be so tired that all you wanted was to lie down, alone, shut off from everyone. And you would snap at your husband, or your children, if they entered the room, probed the solace of your complete surrender to silence and the mattress that seductively held your body. So she understood the baby's helpless sounds for *I want to lie in my crib and put my thumb in my mouth and hold Raggedy Ann's dirty old apron and sleep.* The apron was long removed from the doll, and the baby would not sleep without its presence in her hand. Rose understood this, but could not soothe the baby. She could not have soothed her anyway; only sleep could. But Rose could not try, with hugs, with petting, with her softened voice. She was young.

Perhaps her knowledge of her own failures dulled her ears and eyes to Jim after he first struck the boy, and on that night lost for the rest of his life any paternal control he might have exerted in the past over his hands, finally his fists. Because more and more now he spanked them; with a chill Rose tried to deny, a resonant quiver up through her body, she remembered that her parents had spanked her too. That all, or probably all, parents spanked their children. And usually it was the father, the man of the house, the authority and judge, and enforcer of rules and discipline the children would need when they reached their teens. But now, too, he held them by the shoulders, and shook their small bodies, the children sometimes wailing, sometimes frighteningly silent, until it seemed their heads would fly across the room then roll to rest on the floor, while he shook a body whose neck had snapped in two like a dried branch. He slapped their faces, and sometimes he punched the boy, who was four, then five, with his fist. They were not bad children; not disobedient; certainly they were not loud. When Jim yelled and shook them, or slapped or punched, they had done no more than they had in the supermarket, where her voice, her snatching from their hands, betrayed her to the other women. So maybe that kept her silent.

But there was more: she could no longer feel love, or what she had believed love to be. On the few nights when she and Jim could afford both a sitter and a nightclub, they did not dance. They sat drinking, their talk desultory: about household chores, about Jim's work, pushing wheelbarrows, swinging a sledgehammer, thrusting a spade into the earth or a pile of gravel or sand. They listened to the music, watched the band, even drummed their fingers on the table dampened by the bottoms of the glasses they emptied like thirsty people drinking water; but they thirsted for a time they had lost. Or not even that: for respite from their time now, and their knowledge that, from one day to the next, year after year, their lives would not change. Each day would be like the one they had lived before last night's sleep; and tomorrow was a certain and already draining repetition of today. They did not decide to sit rather than dance. They simply did not dance. They sat and drank and watched the band and the dancing couples, as if their reason for dancing had been stolen from them while their eyes had been jointly focused on something else.

She could no longer feel love. She ate too much and smoked too much and drank too much coffee, so all day she felt either lethargic from eating or stimulated by coffee and cigarettes, and she could not recall her body as it had once been, only a few years ago, when she was dating Jim, and had played softball and volleyball, had danced, and had run into the ocean to swim beyond the breakers. The ocean was a half-hour away from her home, yet she had not seen it in six years. Rather than love, she felt that she and Jim only worked together, exhausted, toward a nebulous end, as if they were digging a large hole, wide as a house, deeper than a well. Side by side they dug, and threw the dirt up and out of the hole, pausing now and then to look at each other, to wait while their breathing slowed, and to feel in those kindred moments something of why they labored, of why they had begun it so long ago—not in years, not long at all—with their dancing and lovemaking and finally marriage: to pause and look at each other's flushed and sweating faces with as much love as they could feel before they commenced again to dig deeper, away from the light above them.

On a summer night in that last year, Jim threw the boy across the living room. Rose was washing the dishes after dinner. Jim was watching television, and the boy, five now, was playing on the floor between Jim and the set. He was on the floor with his sisters and wooden blocks and toy cars and trucks. He seldom spoke directly to his father anymore; seldom spoke at all to anyone but his sisters. The girls were too young, or hopeful, or were still in love. They spoke to Jim, sat on his lap, hugged his legs, and when he hugged them, lifted them in the air, talked with affection and laughter, their faces showed a happiness without memory. And when he yelled at them, or shook or spanked them, or slapped their faces, their memory failed them again, and they were startled, frightened, and Rose could sense their spirits weeping beneath the sounds of their crying. But they kept turning to him, with open arms, and believing faces.

"Little flowers," she said to me. "They were like little flowers in the sun. They never could remember the frost."

Not the boy, though. But that night his game with his sisters absorbed him, and for a short while—nearly an hour—he was a child in a home. He forgot. Several times his father told him and the girls to be quiet or play in another room. Then for a while, a long while for playing children, they were quiet: perhaps five minutes, perhaps ten. Each time their voices rose, Jim's command for quiet was abrupt, and each time it was louder. At the kitchen sink Rose's muscles tensed, told her it was coming, and she must go to the living room now, take the children and their blocks and cars and trucks to the boy's bedroom. But she breathed deeply and rubbed a dish with a sponge. When she finished, she would go down to the basement of the apartment building, descend past the two floors of families and single people whose only sounds were music from radios, voices from television, and sometimes children loudly playing and once in a while a quarrel between a husband and wife. She would go into the damp basement and take the clothes from the washing machine, put them in the dryer that Jim was now paying for with monthly installments. Then she heard his voice again, and was certain it was coming, but could not follow the urging of her muscles. She sponged another dish. Then her hands came out of the dishwater with a glass: it had been a jelly jar, and humanly smiling animals were on it, and flowers, and her children liked to drink from it, looked for it first when they were thirsty, and only if it was dirty in the sink would they settle for an ordinary glass for their water, their juice, or Kool-Aid or milk. She washed it slowly, and was for those moments removed; she was oblivious of the living room, the children's voices rising again to the peak that would bring either Jim's voice or his body from his chair. Her hands moved gently on the glass. She could have been washing one of her babies. Her heart had long ago ceased its signals to her; it lay dormant in despair beyond sorrow; standing at the sink, in a silence of her own making, lightly rubbing the glass with the sponge, and her fingers and palms, she did not know she was crying until the tears reached her lips, salted her tongue.

With their wooden blocks, the children were building a village, and a bridge leading out of it to the country: the open spaces of the living-room carpet, and the chairs and couch that were distant mountains. More adept with his hands, and more absorbed too in the work, the boy often stood to adjust a block on a roof, or the bridge. Each time he stood between his father and the television screen, he heard the quick command, and moved out of the way. They had no slanted blocks, so the bridge had to end with two sheer walls; the boy wanted to build ramps at either end, for the cars and trucks to use, and he had only rectangles and squares to work with. He stood to look down at the bridge. His father spoke. He heard the voice, but a few seconds passed before it penetrated his concentration and spread through him. It was too late. What he heard next was not words, or a roar, but a sustained guttural cry, a sound that could be either anguish or rage. Then his father's hands were on him: on him and squeezing his left thigh and left bicep so tightly that he opened his mouth to cry out in pain. But he did not. For then he was above his father's head, above the floor and his sisters, high above the room itself and near the ceiling he glimpsed; and he felt his father's grip and weight shifting and saw the wall across the room, the wall above the couch, so that when finally he made a sound it was of terror, and it came from him in a high scream he heard as he hurtled across the room, seeing always the wall, and hearing his own scream, as though his flight were prolonged by the horror of what he saw and heard. Then he struck it. He heard that, and the bone in his right forearm snap, and he fell to the couch. Now he cried with pain, staring at the swollen flesh where the bone tried to protrude, staring with astonishment and grief at this part of his body. Nothing in his body had ever broken before. He touched the flesh, the bone beneath it. He was crying as, in his memory, he had never cried before, and he not only did not try to stop, as he always had, with pride, with anger; but he wanted to cry this deeply, his body shuddering with it, doubling at his waist with it, until he attained oblivion, invisibility, death. Somehow he knew his childhood had ended. In his pain, he felt relief too: now on this couch his life would end.

He saw through tears but more strongly felt his sisters standing before him, touching him, crying. Then he heard his mother. She was screaming. And in rage. At his father. He had never heard her do that, but still her scream did not come to him as a saving trumpet. He did not want to live to see revenge. Not even victory. Then he heard his father slap her. Through his crying he listened then for her silence. But her voice grew, its volume filled the world. Still he felt nothing of hope, of vengeance; he had left that world, and lived now for what he hoped and believed would be only a very short time. He was beginning to feel the pain in his head and back and shoulders, his elbows and neck. He knew he would only have to linger a while in this pain, until his heart left him, as though disgorged by tears, and went wherever hearts went. A sister's hand held his, and he squeezed it.

When he was above his father's head, the boy had not seen Rose. But she was there, behind Jim, behind the lifted boy, and she had cried out too, and moved: as Jim regained his balance from throwing the boy, she turned him, her hand jerking his shoulder, and when she could see his face she pounded it with her fists. She was yelling, and the yell was words, but she did not know what they were. She hit him until he pushed her back, hard, so she nearly fell. She looked at his face, the cheeks reddened by her blows, saw a trickle of blood from his lower lip, and charged it: swinging at the blood, the lip. He slapped her so hard that she was sitting on the floor, with no memory of falling, and holding and shaking her stunned and buzzing head. She stood, yelling words again that she could not hear, as if their utterance had been so long coming, from whatever depth in her, that her mind could not even record them as they rushed through her lips. She went past Jim, pushing his belly, and he fell backward into his chair. She paused to look at that. Her breath was deep and fast, and he sat glaring, his breathing hard too, and she neither knew nor cared whether he had desisted or was preparing himself for more. At the bottom of her vision, she saw his beer bottle on the floor beside the chair. She snatched it up, by its neck, beer hissing onto her arm and breast, and in one motion she turned away from Jim and flung the bottle smashing through the television screen. He was up and yelling behind her, but she was crouched over the boy.

She felt again what she had felt in the kitchen, in the silence she had made for herself while she bathed the glass. Behind and above her was the sound of Jim's fury; yet she stroked the boy's face: his forehead, the tears beneath his eyes; she touched the girls too, their hair, their wet faces; and she heard her own voice: soft and soothing, so soft and soothing that she even believed the peace it promised. Then she saw, beneath the boy's hand, the swollen flesh; gently she lifted his hand, then was on her feet. She stood into Jim's presence again: his voice behind her, the feel of his large body inches from her back. Then he gripped her hair, at the back of her head, and she shook her head but still he held on.

"His *arm's* broken."

She ran from him, felt hair pulling from her scalp, heard it, and ran to her bedroom for her purse but not a blanket, not from the bed where she slept with Jim; for that she went to the boy's, and pulled his thin summer blanket from his bed, and ran back to the living room. Where she stopped. Jim stood at the couch, not looking at the boy, or the girls, but at the doorway where now she stood holding the blanket. He was waiting for her.

"You crazy fucking bitch."

"What?"

"The fucking TV. Who's going to buy one? You? You fucking cunt. You've never had a fucking job in your life."

It was madness. She was looking at madness, and it calmed her. She had nothing to say to it. She went to the couch, opening the blanket to wrap around the boy.

"It's the only fucking peace I've *got.*"

She heard him, but it was like overhearing someone else, in another apartment, another life. She crouched and was working the blanket under the boy's body when a fist knocked loudly on the door. She did not pause, or look up. More knocking, then a voice in the hall: "Hey! Everybody all right in there?"

"Get the fuck away from my door."

"You tell me everybody's all right."

"Get the fuck *away.*"

"I want to hear the woman. And the kid."

"You want me to throw you down the fucking stairs?"

"I'm calling the cops."

"Fuck you."

She had the boy in her arms now. He was crying still, and as she carried him past Jim, she kissed his cheeks, his eyes. Then Jim was beside her. He opened the door, swung it back for them. She did not realize until weeks later that he was frightened. His voice was low: "Tell them he fell."

She did not answer. She went out and down the stairs, past apartments; in one of them someone was phoning the police. At the bottom of the stairs she stopped short of the door, to shift the boy's weight in her arms, to free a hand for the knob. Then an old woman stepped out of her apartment, into the hall, and said: "I'll get it."

An old woman with white hair and a face that knew everything, not only tonight, but the years before this too, yet the face was neither stern nor kind; it looked at Rose with some tolerant recognition of evil, of madness, of despair, like a warrior who has seen and done too much to condemn, or even try to judge; can only nod in assent at what he sees. The woman opened the door and held it, and Rose went out, across the small lawn to the car parked on the road. There were only two other cars at the curb; then she remembered that it was Saturday, and had been hot, and before noon she had heard most of the tenants separately leaving for beaches or picnic grounds. They would be driving home now, or stopping to eat. The sun had just set, but most windows of the tenements on the street were dark. She stopped at the passenger door, started to shift the weeping boy's weight, then the old woman was beside her, trying the door, asking for the key. Rose's purse hung from her wrist. The woman's hands went into it, moved in there, came out with the ring of keys, held them up toward the streetlight, and found the one for the car. She opened the door, and Rose leaned in and laid the boy on the front seat. She turned to thank the woman but she was already at the front door of the building, a square back and short body topped by hair like cotton.

Rose gently closed the car door, holding it, making certain it was not touching the boy before she pushed it into place. She ran to the driver's side, and got in, and put the key in the ignition slot. But she could not turn it. She sat in the boy's crying, poised in the moment of action the car had become. But she could not start it.

"Jimmy," she said. "Jimmy, listen. Just hang on. I'll be right back. I can't leave the girls. Do you hear me?"

His face, profiled on the seat, nodded.

"I've got to get them."

She pushed open the door, left the car, closed the door, the keys in her hands, not out of habit this time; no, she clung to them as she might to a tiny weapon, her last chance to be saved. She was running to the building when she saw the flames at her windows, a flare of them where an instant before there had been only lamplight. Her legs now, her body, were weightless as the wind. She heard the girls screaming. Then the front door opened and Jim ran out of it, collided with her, and she fell on her back as he stumbled and side-stepped and tried to regain balance and speed and go around her. Her left hand grabbed his left ankle. Then she turned with his pulling, his weight, and, on her stomach now, she held his ankle with her right hand too, and pulled it back and up. He fell. She dived onto his back, saw and smelled the gasoline can in his hand, and in her mind she saw him going down to the basement for it, and back up the stairs. She twisted it away from his fingers on the handle, and kneeled with his back between her legs, and as he lifted his head and shoulders and tried to stand, she raised the can high with both hands and brought it down, leaning with it, into it, as it struck his skull. For a moment he was still, his face in the grass. Then he began to struggle again, and said into the earth: "Over now. All over."

She hit him three more times, the sounds hollow, metallic. Then he was still, save for the rise and fall of his back. Beneath his other hand she saw his set of car keys. She scooped them from the grass and stood and threw them across the lawn, whirling now into the screams of the girls, and windows of fire. She ran up the stairs. The white-haired woman was on the second-floor landing. Rose passed her, felt her following, and the others: she did not know how many, nor who they were. She only heard them behind her. No one passed her. She was at the door, trying to turn the knob, while her left arm and hand pressed hot wood.

"I called the fire department," a man said, behind her in the hall.

"So did we," a woman said.

Rose was calling to the girls to open the door,

"They can't," another man said. "That's where the fire is." Then he said: "Fuck this," and pulled her away from the door where she was turning the knob back and forth and calling through the wood to the screams from the rear of the apartment, their bedroom. She was about to spring back to the door, but stopped: the man faced it, then stepped away. She knew his name, or had known it; she could not say it. He lived on the second floor; it was his wife who had said *So did we.* He stepped twice toward the door, then kicked, his leg horizontal, the bottom of his shoe striking the door, and it swung open, through the flames that filled the threshold and climbed the doorjambs. The man leaped backward, his forearms covering his face, while Rose yelled to the girls: *We're coming, we're coming.* The man lowered his head and sprinted forward. Or it would have been a sprint. Certainly he believed that, believed he would run through fire to the girls and get them out. But in his third stride his legs stopped, so suddenly and autonomously that he nearly fell forward into the fire. Then he backed up.

"They'll have a net," he said. He was panting. "We'll get them to jump. We'll get them to a window, and get them to jump."

A man behind Rose was holding her. She had not known it till now. Nor had she known she was straining forward. The man tightly held her biceps. He was talking to her and now she heard that too, and was also aware that people were moving away, slowly but away, down the hall toward the stairs. He was saying, "You can't. All you'll do is get yourself killed."

Then she was out of his hands, as though his fingers were those of a child, and, with her breath held and her arms shielding her face, and her head down, she was in motion, through the flames and into the burning living room. She did not feel the fire, but even as she ran through the living room, dodging flames, running through them, she knew that very soon she would. It meant no more to her than knowing that she was getting wet in a sudden rain. The girls were standing on the older one's bed, at the far side of the room, holding each other, screaming, and watching their door and the hall beyond it where the fire would come. She filled the door, their vision, then was at the bed and they were crying: *Mommy! Mommy!* She did not speak. She did not touch them either. She pulled the blanket from under them, and they fell onto the bed. Running again, she grabbed the blanket from the younger girl's bed, and went into the hall where there was smoke but not fire yet, and across it to the bathroom where she turned on the shower and held the blankets under the spray. They soaked heavily in her hands. She held her breath leaving the bathroom and exhaled in the girls' room. They were standing again, holding each other. Now she spoke to them. Again, as when she had crouched with them in front of Jimmy, her voice somehow came softly from her. It was unhurried, calm, soothing: she could have been helping them put on snowsuits. They stopped screaming, even crying; they only sniffled and gasped as she wound a blanket around each of them, covering their feet and heads too, then lifted them, pressing one to each breast. Then she stopped talking, stopped telling them that very soon, before they even knew it, they would be safe outside. She turned and ran through smoke in the hall, and into the living room. She did not try to dodge flames: if they were in front of her, she spun and ran backward through them, hugging the girls against each other, so nothing of their bodies would protude past her back, her sides; then spun and ran forward again, fearful of an image that entered her mind, though in an instant she expelled it: that she would fall with them, into fire. She ran backward through the door, and her back hit the wall. She bounced off it; there was fire in the hall now, moving at her ankles, and she ran, leaping, and when she reached the stairs she smelled the scorched blankets that steamed around the girls in her arms. She smelled her burned hair, sensed that it was burning still, crackling flames on her head. It could wait. She could wait. She was running down the stairs, and the fire was behind her, above her, and she felt she could run with her girls all night. Then she was on the lawn, and arms took the girls, and a man wrestled her to the ground and rolled with her, rolled over and over on the grass. When she stood, someone was telling her an ambulance would— But she picked up her girls, unwrapped now, and looked at their faces: pale with terror, with shock, yes; but no burns. She carried them to the car.

"*No*," she heard. It was a man's voice, but one she did not know. Not for a few moments, as she laid the girls side by side on the back seat. Then she knew it was Jim. She was startled, as though she had not seen him for ten years. She ran around the car, got behind the wheel, reached over Jimmy, who was silent now and she thought unconscious until she saw his eyes staring at the dashboard, his teeth gritting against his pain. Leaning over his face, she pushed down the latch on his side. Then she locked her door. It was a two-door car, and they were safe now and they were going to the hospital. She started the engine.

Jim was at her window, a raging face, but a desperate one too, as though standing outside he was locked in a room without air. Then he was motion, on her left, to her front, and he stood at the middle of the car, slapped his hands onto the hood, and pushed. He bulged: his arms and chest and reddened face. With all his strength he pushed, and she felt the car rock backward. She turned on the head-lights. The car rocked forward as he eased his pushing and drew breath. Then he pushed again, leaning, so all she could see of him was his face, his shoulders, his arms. The car rocked back and stopped. She pushed the accelerator pedal to the floor, waited two or three seconds in which she either did not breathe or held what breath she had, and watched his face above the sound of the raging engine. Then, in one quick motion, she lifted her foot from the clutch pedal. He was gone as she felt the bumper and grille leap through his resistance. She stopped and looked in the rear-view mirror; she saw the backs of the girls' heads, their long hair; they were kneeling on the seat, looking quietly out the back window. He lay on his back. Rose turned her wheels to the right, as though to back into a parking space, shifted to reverse, and this time without racing the engine, she slowly drove. She did not look through the rear window; she looked straight ahead, at the street, the tenements, the darkening sky. Only the rear tires rolled over him, then struck the curb. She straightened the front wheels and drove forward again. The car bumped over him. She stopped, shifted gears, and backed up: the bump, then the tires hitting the curb. She was still driving back and forth over his body, while beyond her closed windows people shouted or stared, when the sirens broke the summer sky: the higher wail of the police called by the neighbor, and the lower and louder one of the fire engine.

She was in the hospital, and by the time she got out, her three brothers and two sisters had found money for bail. Her parents were dead. Waiting for the trial, she lived with a married sister; there were children in the house, and Rose shied away from them. Her court-appointed lawyer called it justifiable homicide, and the jury agreed. Long before the trial, before she even left the hospital, she had lost the children. The last time she saw them was that night in the car, when finally she took them away: the boy lying on the front seat, his left cheek resting on it as he stared. He did not move while she drove back and forth over his father. She still does not know whether he knew then, or learned it from his sisters. And the two girls kneeling, their chests leaning on the back of the seat, watching their father appear, then vanish as a bump beneath them. They all went to the same foster home. She did not know where it was.

"Thanks for the drinks," she said, and patted my hand. "Next time you're broke, let me know."

"I will."

She adjusted the blue scaf over her hair, knotted it under her face, buttoned her coat, and put on her gloves. She stepped away from the bar, and walked around and between people. I ordered a beer, and watched her go out the door. I paid and tipped Steve, then left the bottle and glass with my coat and hat on the bar, and moved through the crowd. I stepped outside and watched her, a half-block away now. She was walking carefully in the lightly falling snow, her head down, watching the sidewalk, and I remembered her eyes when she talked about slipping on ice. But what had she been sharing with me? Age?

Death? I don't think so. I believe it was the unexpected: chance, and its indiscriminate testing of our bodies, our wills, our spirits. She was walking toward the bridge over the Merrimack. It is a long bridge, and crossing it in that open air she would be cold. I was shivering. She was at the bridge now, her silhouette diminishing as she walked on it. I watched until she disappeared.

I had asked her if she had tried to find her children, had tried an appeal to get them back. She did not deserve them, she said. And after the testimony of her neighbors, she knew she had little hope anyway. She should have hit him with the skillet, she said; the first time he slapped the boy. I said nothing. As I have written, we have talked often since then, but we do not mention her history, and she does not ask for mine, though I know she guesses some of it. All of this is blurred; nothing stands out with purity. By talking to social workers, her neighbors condemned her to lose her children; talking in the courtroom, they helped save her from conviction.

I imagine again those men long ago, sitting among mosquitoes in a room, or sleeping on the fouled sheets. Certainly each of them hoped that it was not the mosquito biting his arm, or the bed he slept on, that would end his life. So he hoped for the men in the other room to die. Unless he hoped that it was neither sheets nor mosquitoes, but then he would be hoping for the experiment to fail, for yellow fever to flourish. And he had volunteered to stop it. Perhaps though, among those men, there was one, or even more, who hoped that he alone would die, and his death would be a discovery for all.

The boy from Chicago and Rose were volunteers too. I hope that by now the man from Chicago has succeeded at something—love, work—that has allowed him to outgrow the shame of failure. I have often imagined him returning home a week early that summer, to a mother, to a father; and having to watch his father's face as the boy told him he had failed because he was weak. A trifling incident in a whole lifetime, you may say. Not true. It could have changed him forever, his life with other men, with women, with daughters, and especially sons. We like to believe that in this last quarter of the century, we know and are untouched by everything; yet it takes only a very small jolt, at the right time, to knock us off balance for the rest of our lives. Maybe—and I hope so—the boy learned what his body and will could do: some occurrence he did not have time to consider, something that made him act before he knew he was in action.

Like Rose. Who volunteered to marry; even, to a degree, to practice rhythm, for her Catholic beliefs were not strong and deep, else she could not have so easily turned away from them after the third child, or even early in that pregnancy. So the life she chose slowly turned on her, pressed against her from all sides, invisible, motionless, but with the force of wind she could not breast. She stood at the sink, holding the children's glass. But *then*—and now finally I know why I write this, and what does stand out with purity—she reentered motherhood, and the unity we all must gain against human suffering. This is why I did not answer, at the bar, when she told me she did not deserve the children. For I believe she did, and does. She redeemed herself, with action, and with less than thirty minutes of it. But she could not see that, and still cannot. She sees herself in the laundromat, the supermarket, listlessly drunk in a nightclub where only her fingers on the table moved to the music. I see her young and strong and swift, wrapping the soaked blankets around her little girls, and hugging them to her, and running and spinning and running through the living room, on that summer night when she was touched and blessed by flames.

THE FAT GIRL

Her name was Louise. Once when she was sixteen a boy kissed her at a barbecue; he was drunk and he jammed his tongue into her mouth and ran his hands up and down her hips. Her father kissed her often. He was thin and kind and she could see in his eyes when he looked at her the lights of love and pity.

It started when Louise was nine. You must start watching what you eat, her mother would say. I can see you have my metabolism. Louise also had her mother's pale blonde hair. Her mother was slim and pretty, carried herself erectly, and ate very little. The two of them would eat bare lunches, while her older brother ate sandwiches and potato chips, and then her mother would sit smoking while Louise eyed the bread box, the pantry, the refrigerator. Wasn't that good, her mother would say. In five years you'll be in high school and if you're fat the boys won't like you; they won't ask you out. Boys were as far away as five years, and she would go to her room and wait for nearly an hour until she knew her mother was no longer thinking of her, then she would creep into the kitchen and, listening to her mother talking on the phone, or her footsteps upstairs, she would open the bread box, the pantry, the jar of peanut butter. She would put the sandwich under her shirt and go outside or to the bathroom to eat it.

Her father was a lawyer and made a lot of money and came home looking pale and happy. Martinis put color back in his face, and at dinner he talked to his wife and two children. Oh give her a potato, he would say to Louise's mother. She's a growing girl. Her mother's voice then became tense: If she has a potato she shouldn't have dessert. She should have both, her father would say, and he would reach over and touch Louise's cheek or hand or arm.

In high school she had two girl friends and at night and on weekends they rode in a car or went to movies. In movies she was fascinated by fat actresses. She wondered why they were fat. She knew why she was fat: she was fat because she was Louise. Because God had made her that way. Because she wasn't like her friends Joan and Marjorie, who drank milk shakes after school and were all bones and tight skin. But what about those actresses, with their talents, with their broad and profound faces? Did they eat as heedlessly as Bishop Humphries and his wife who sometimes came to dinner and, as Louise's mother said, gorged between amenities? Or did they try to lose weight, did they go about hungry and angry and thinking of food? She thought of them eating lean meats and salads with friends, and then going home and building strange large sandwiches with French bread. But mostly she believed they did not go through these failures; they were fat because they chose to be. And she was certain of something else too: she could see it in their faces: they did not eat secretly. Which she did: her creeping to the kitchen when she was nine became, in high school, a ritual of deceit and pleasure. She was a furtive eater of sweets. Even her two friends did not know her secret.

Joan was thin, gangling, and flat-chested; she was attractive enough and all she needed was someone to take a second look at her face, but the school was large and there were pretty girls in every classroom and walking all the corridors, so no one ever needed to take a second look at Joan. Marjorie was thin too, an intense, heavy-smoking girl with brittle laughter. She was very intelligent, and with boys she was shy because she knew she made them uncomfortable, and because she was smarter than they were and so could not understand or could not believe the levels they lived on. She was to have a nervous breakdown before earning her Ph.D. in philosophy at the University of California, where she met and married a physicist and discovered within herself an untrammelled passion: she made love with her husband on the couch, the carpet, in the bathtub, and on the washing machine. By that time much had happened to her and she never thought of Louise. Joan would finally stop growing and begin moving with grace and confidence. In college she would have two lovers and then several more during the six years she spent in Boston before marrying a middle-aged editor who had two sons in their early teens, who drank too much, who was tenderly, boyishly grateful for her love, and whose wife had been killed while rock-climbing in New Hampshire with her lover. She would not think of Louise either, except in an earlier time, when lovers were still new to her and she was ecstatically surprised each time one of them loved her and, sometimes at night, lying in a man's arms, she would tell how in high school no one dated her, she had been thin and plain (she would still believe that: that she had been plain; it had never been true) and so had been forced into the weekend and night-time company of a neurotic smart girl and a shy fat girl. She would say this with self-pity exaggerated by Scotch and her need to be more deeply loved by the man who held her.

She never eats, Joan and Marjorie said of Louise. They ate lunch with her at school, watched her refusing potatoes, ravioli, fried fish. Sometimes she got through the cafeteria line with only a salad. That is how they would remember her: a girl whose hapless body was destined to be fat. No one saw the sandwiches she made and took to her room when she came home from school. No one saw the store of Milky Ways, Butterfingers, Almond Joys, and Hersheys far back on her closet shelf, behind the stuffed animals of her childhood. She was not a hypocrite. When she was out of the house she truly believed she was dieting; she forgot about the candy, as a man speaking into his office dictaphone may forget the lewd photographs hidden in an old shoe in his closet. At other times, away from home, she thought of the waiting candy with near lust. One night driving home from a movie, Majorie said: "You're lucky you don't smoke; it's in*cred*ible what I go through to hide it from my parents." Louise turned to her a smile which was elusive and mysterious; she yearned to be home in bed, eating chocolate in the dark. She did not need to smoke; she already had a vice that was insular and destructive.

She brought it with her to college. She thought she would leave it behind. A move from one place to another, a new room without the haunted closet shelf, would do for her what she could not do for herself. She packed her large dresses and went. For two weeks she was busy with registration, with shyness, with classes; then she began to feel at home. Her room was no longer like a motel. Its walls had stopped watching her, she felt they were her friends, and she gave them her secret. Away from her mother, she did not have to be as elaborate; she kept the candy in her drawer now.

The school was in Massachusetts, a girls' school. When she chose it, when she and her father and mother talked about it in the evenings, everyone so carefully avoided the word boys that sometimes the conversations seemed to be about nothing but boys. There are no boys there, the neuter words said; you will not have to contend with that. In her father's eyes were pity and encouragement; in her mother's was disappointment, and her voice was crisp. They spoke of courses, of small classes where Louise would get more attention. She imagined herself in those small classes; she saw herself as a teacher would see her, as the other girls would; she would get no attention.

The girls at the school were from wealthy families, but most of them wore the uniform of another class: blue jeans and work shirts, and many wore overalls. Louise bought some overalls, washed them until the dark blue faded, and wore them to classes. In the cafeteria she ate as she had in high school, not to lose weight nor even to sus-

tain her lie, but because eating lightly in public had become as habit-
ual as good manners. Everyone had to take gym, and in the locker
room with the other girls, and wearing shorts on the volleyball and
badminton courts, she hated her body. She liked her body most when
she was unaware of it: in bed at night, as sleep gently took her out of
her day, out of herself. And she liked parts of her body. She liked her
brown eyes and sometimes looked at them in the mirror: they were
not shallow eyes, she thought; they were indeed windows of a tender
soul, a good heart. She liked her lips and nose, and her chin, finely
shaped between her wide and sagging cheeks. Most of all she liked
her long pale blonde hair, she liked washing and drying it and lying
naked on her bed, smelling of shampoo, and feeling the soft hair at
her neck and shoulders and back.

Her friend at college was Carrie, who was thin and wore thick
glasses and often at night she cried in Louise's room. She did not
know why she was crying. She was crying, she said, because she was
unhappy. She could say no more. Louise said she was unhappy too,
and Carrie moved in with her. One night Carrie talked for hours,
sadly and bitterly, about her parents and what they did to each other.
When she finished she hugged Louise and they went to bed. Then
in the dark Carrie spoke across the room: "Louise? I just wanted to
tell you. One night last week I woke up and smelled chocolate. You
were eating chocolate, in your bed. I wish you'd eat it in front of me,
Louise, whenever you feel like it."

Stiffened in her bed, Louise could think of nothing to say. In the
silence she was afraid Carrie would think she was asleep and would
tell her again in the morning or tomorrow night. Finally she said
Okay. Then after a moment she told Carrie if she ever wanted any
she could feel free to help herself; the candy was in the top drawer.
Then she said thank you.

They were roommates for four years and in the summers they
exchanged letters. Each fall they greeted with embraces, laughter,
tears, and moved into their old room, which had been stripped and
cleansed of them for the summer. Neither girl enjoyed summer. Car-

rie did not like being at home because her parents did not love each other. Louise lived in a small city in Louisiana. She did not like summer because she had lost touch with Joan and Marjorie; they saw each other, but it was not the same. She liked being with her father but with no one else. The flicker of disappointment in her mother's eyes at the airport was a vanguard of the army of relatives and acquaintances who awaited her: they would see her on the streets, in stores, at the country club, in her home, and in theirs; in the first moments of greeting, their eyes would tell her she was still fat Louise, who had been fat as long as they could remember, who had gone to college and returned as fat as ever. Then their eyes dismissed her, and she longed for school and Carrie, and she wrote letters to her friend. But that saddened her too. It wasn't simply that Carrie was her only friend, and when they finished college they might never see each other again. It was that her existence in the world was so divided; it had begun when she was a child creeping to the kitchen; now that division was much sharper, and her friendship with Carrie seemed disproportionate and perilous. The world she was destined to live in had nothing to do with the intimate nights in their room at school.

In the summer before their senior year, Carrie fell in love. She wrote to Louise about him, but she did not write much, and this hurt Louise more than if Carrie had shown the joy her writing tried to conceal. That fall they returned to their room; they were still close and warm, Carrie still needed Louise's ears and heart at night as she spoke of her parents and her recurring malaise whose source the two friends never discovered. But on most week-ends Carrie left, and caught a bus to Boston where her boyfriend studied music. During the week she often spoke hesitantly of sex; she was not sure if she liked it. But Louise, eating candy and listening, did not know whether Carrie was telling the truth or whether, as in her letters of the past summer, Carrie was keeping from her those delights she may never experience.

Then one Sunday night when Carrie had just returned from Boston and was unpacking her overnight bag, she looked at Louise and said: "I was thinking about you. On the bus coming home tonight." Looking at Carrie's concerned, determined face, Louise prepared herself for humiliation. "I was thinking about when we graduate. What you're going to do. What's to become of you. I want you to be loved the way I love you. Louise, if I help you, *rea*lly help you, will you go on a diet?"

Louise entered a period of her life she would remember always, the way some people remember having endured poverty. Her diet did not begin the next day. Carrie told her to eat on Monday as though it were the last day of her life. So for the first time since grammar school Louise went into a school cafeteria and ate everything she wanted. At breakfast and lunch and dinner she glanced around the table to see if the other girls noticed the food on her tray. They did not. She felt there was a lesson in this, but it lay beyond her grasp. That night in their room she ate the four remaining candy bars. During the day Carrie rented a small refrigerator, bought an electric skillet, an electric broiler, and bathroom scales.

On Tuesday morning Louise stood on the scales, and Carrie wrote in her notebook: *October 14: 184 lbs.* Then she made Louise a cup of black coffee and scrambled one egg and sat with her while she ate. When Carrie went to the dining room for breakfast, Louise walked about the campus for thirty minutes. That was part of the plan. The campus was pretty, on its lawns grew at least one of every tree native to New England, and in the warm morning sun Louise felt a new hope. At noon they met in their room, and Carrie broiled her a piece of hamburger and served it with lettuce. Then while Carrie ate in the dining room Louise walked again. She was weak with hunger and she felt queasy. During her afternoon classes she was nervous and tense, and she chewed her pencil and tapped her heels on the floor and tightened her calves. When she returned to her room late that afternoon, she was so glad to see Carrie that she embraced her; she had felt she could not bear another minute of hunger, but now with Carrie she knew she could make it at least through tonight. Then she would sleep and face tomorrow when it came. Carrie broiled her a steak and served it with lettuce. Louise studied while Carrie ate dinner, then they went for a walk.

That was her ritual and her diet for the rest of the year, Carrie alternating fish and chicken breasts with the steaks for dinner, and every day was nearly as bad as the first. In the evenings she was irritable. In all her life she had never been afflicted by ill temper and she looked upon it now as a demon which, along with hunger, was taking possession of her soul. Often she spoke sharply to Carrie. One night during their after-dinner walk Carrie talked sadly of night, of how darkness made her more aware of herself, and at night she did not know why she was in college, why she studied, why she was walking the earth with other people. They were standing on a wooden foot bridge, looking down at a dark pond. Carrie kept talking; perhaps soon she would cry. Suddenly Louise said: "I'm sick of lettuce. I never want to see a piece of lettuce for the rest of my life. I hate it. We shouldn't even buy it, it's immoral."

Carrie was quiet. Louise glanced at her, and the pain and irritation in Carrie's face soothed her. Then she was ashamed. Before she could say she was sorry, Carrie turned to her and said gently: "I know. I know how terrible it is."

Carrie did all the shopping, telling Louise she knew how hard it was to go into a supermarket when you were hungry. And Louise was always hungry. She drank diet soft drinks and started smoking Carrie's cigarettes, learned to enjoy inhaling, thought of cancer and emphysema but they were as far away as those boys her mother had talked about when she was nine. By Thanksgiving she was smoking over a pack a day and her weight in Carrie's notebook was one hundred and sixty-two pounds. Carrie was afraid if Louise went home at Thanksgiving she would lapse from the diet, so Louise spent the vacation with Carrie, in Philadelphia. Carrie wrote her family about the diet, and told Louise that she had. On the plane to Philadelphia,

Louise said: "I feel like a bedwetter. When I was a little girl I had a friend who used to come spend the night and Mother would put a rubber sheet on the bed and we all pretended there wasn't a rubber sheet and that she hadn't wet the bed. Even me, and I slept with her." At Thanksgiving dinner she lowered her eyes as Carrie's father put two slices of white meat on her plate and passed it to her over the bowls of steaming food.

When she went home at Christmas she weighed a hundred and fifty-five pounds; at the airport her mother marvelled. Her father laughed and hugged her and said: "But now there's less of you to love." He was troubled by her smoking but only mentioned it once; he told her she was beautiful and, as always, his eyes bathed her with love. During the long vacation her mother cooked for her as Carrie had, and Louise returned to school weighing a hundred and forty-six pounds.

Flying north on the plane she warmly recalled the surprised and congratulatory eyes of her relatives and acquaintances. She had not seen Joan or Marjorie. She thought of returning home in May, weighing the hundred and fifteen pounds which Carrie had in October set as their goal. Looking toward the stoic days ahead, she felt strong. She thought of those hungry days of fall and early winter (and now: she was hungry now: with almost a frown, almost a brusque shake of the head, she refused peanuts from the stewardess): those first weeks of the diet when she was the pawn of an irascibility which still, conditioned to her ritual as she was, could at any moment take command of her. She thought of the nights of trying to sleep while her stomach growled. She thought of her addiction to cigarettes. She thought of the people at school: not one teacher, not one girl, had spoken to her about her loss of weight, not even about her absence from meals. And without warning her spirit collapsed. She did not feel strong, she did not feel she was committed to and within reach of achieving a valuable goal. She felt that somehow she had lost more than pounds of fat; that some time during her dieting she had lost herself too. She tried to remember what it had felt like to be Louise before she had started living on meat and fish, as an unhappy adult may look sadly in the memory of childhood for lost virtues and hopes. She looked down at the earth far below, and it seemed to her that her soul, like her body aboard the plane, was in some rootless flight. She neither knew its destination nor where it had departed from; it was on some passage she could not even define.

During the next few weeks she lost weight more slowly and once for eight days Carrie's daily recording stayed at a hundred and thirty-six. Louise woke in the morning thinking of one hundred and thirty-six and then she stood on the scales and they echoed her. She became obsessed with that number, and there wasn't a day when she didn't say it aloud, and through the days and nights the number stayed in her mind, and if a teacher had spoken those digits in a classroom she would have opened her mouth to speak. What if that's me, she said to Carrie. I mean what if a hundred and thirty-six is my real weight and I just can't lose any more. Walking hand-in-hand with her despair was a longing for this to be true, and that longing angered her and wearied her, and every day she was gloomy. On the ninth day she weighed a hundred and thirty-five and a half pounds. She was not relieved; she thought bitterly of the months ahead, the shedding of the last twenty and a half pounds.

On Easter Sunday, which she spent at Carrie's, she weighed one hundred and twenty pounds, and she ate one slice of glazed pineapple with her ham and lettuce. She did not enjoy it: she felt she was being friendly with a recalcitrant enemy who had once tried to destroy her. Carrie's parents were laudative. She liked them and she wished they would touch sometimes, and look at each other when they spoke. She guessed they would divorce when Carrie left home, and she vowed that her own marriage would be one of affection and tenderness. She could think about that now: marriage. At school she had read in a Boston paper that this summer the cicadas would come out of their seventeen year hibernation on Cape Cod, for a month they would mate and then die, leaving their young to burrow into the ground where they would stay for seventeen years. That's me, she had said to Carrie. Only my hibernation lasted twenty-one years.

Often her mother asked in letters and on the phone about the diet, but Louise answered vaguely. When she flew home in late May she weighed a hundred and thirteen pounds, and at the airport her mother cried and hugged her and said again and again: You're so *beauti*ful. Her father blushed and bought her a martini. For days her relatives and acquaintances congratulated her, and the applause in their eyes lasted the entire summer, and she loved their eyes, and swam in the country club pool, the first time she had done this since she was a child.

She lived at home and ate the way her mother did and every morning she weighed herself on the scales in her bathroom. Her mother liked to take her shopping and buy her dresses and they put her old ones in the Goodwill box at the shopping center; Louise thought of them existing on the body of a poor woman whose cheap meals kept her fat. Louise's mother had a photographer come to the house, and Louise posed on the couch and standing beneath a live oak and sitting in a wicker lawn chair next to an azalea bush. The new clothes and the photographer made her feel she was going to another country or becoming a citizen of a new one. In the fall she took a job of no consequence, to give herself something to do.

Also in the fall a young lawyer joined her father's firm, he came one night to dinner, and they started seeing each other. He was the first man outside her family to kiss her since the barbecue when she was sixteen. Louise celebrated Thanksgiving not with rice dressing and candied sweet potatoes and mince meat and pumpkin pies, but by giving Richard her virginity which she realized, at the very last moment of its existence, she had embarked on giving him over thirteen months ago, on that Tuesday in October when Carrie had made her a cup of black coffee and scrambled one egg. She wrote this to

Carrie, who replied happily by return mail. She also, through glance and smile and innuendo, tried to tell her mother too. But finally she controlled that impulse, because Richard felt guilty about making love with the daughter of his partner and friend. In the spring they married. The wedding was a large one, in the Episcopal church, and Carrie flew from Boston to be maid of honor. Her parents had recently separated and she was living with the musician and was still victim of her unpredictable malaise. It overcame her on the night before the wedding, so Louise was up with her until past three and woke next morning from a sleep so heavy that she did not want to leave it.

Richard was a lean, tall, energetic man with the metabolism of a pencil sharpener. Louise fed him everything he wanted. He liked Italian food and she got recipes from her mother and watched him eating spaghetti with the sauce she had only tasted, and ravioli and lasagna, while she ate antipasto with her chianti. He made a lot of money and borrowed more and they bought a house whose lawn sloped down to the shore of a lake; they had a wharf and a boathouse, and Richard bought a boat and they took friends waterskiing. Richard bought her a car and they spent his vacations in Mexico, Canada, the Bahamas, and in the fifth year of their marriage they went to Europe and, according to their plan, she conceived a child in Paris. On the plane back, as she looked out the window and beyond the sparkling sea and saw her country, she felt that it was waiting for her, as her home by the lake was, and her parents, and her good friends who rode in the boat and waterskied; she thought of the accumulated warmth and pelf of her marriage, and how by slimming her body she had bought into the pleasures of the nation. She felt cunning, and she smiled to herself, and took Richard's hand.

But these moments of triumph were sparse. On most days she went about her routine of leisure with a sense of certainty about herself that came merely from not thinking. But there were times, with her friends, or with Richard, or alone in the house, when she was suddenly assaulted by the feeling that she had taken the wrong train and arrived at a place where no one knew her, and where she ought not to be. Often, in bed with Richard, she talked of being fat: "I was the one who started the friendship with Carrie, I chose her, I started the conversations. When I understood that she was my friend I understood something else: I had chosen her for the same reason I'd chosen Joan and Marjorie. They were all thin. I was always thinking about what people saw when they looked at me and I didn't want them to see two fat girls. When I was alone I didn't mind being fat but then I'd have to leave the house again and then I didn't want to look like me. But at home I didn't mind except when I was getting dressed to go out of the house and when Mother looked at me. But I stopped looking at her when she looked at me. And in college I felt good with Carrie; there weren't any boys and I didn't have any other friends and so when I wasn't with Carrie I thought about her and I tried to ignore the other people around me, I tried to make them not exist. A lot of the time I could do that. It was strange, and I felt like a spy."

If Richard was bored by her repetition he pretended not to be. But she knew the story meant very little to him. She could have been telling him of a childhood illness, or wearing braces, or a broken heart at sixteen. He could not see her as she was when she was fat. She felt as though she were trying to tell a foreign lover about her life in the United States, and if only she could command the language he would know and love all of her and she would feel complete. Some of the acquaintances of her childhood were her friends now, and even they did not seem to remember her when she was fat.

Now her body was growing again, and when she put on a maternity dress for the first time she shivered with fear. Richard did not smoke and he asked her, in a voice just short of demand, to stop during her pregnancy. She did. She ate carrots and celery instead of smoking, and at cocktail parties she tried to eat nothing, but after her first drink she ate nuts and cheese and crackers and dips. Always at these parties Richard had talked with his friends and she had rarely spoken to him until they drove home. But now when he noticed her at the hors d'oeuvres table he crossed the room and, smiling, led her back to his group. His smile and his hand on her arm told her he was doing his clumsy, husbandly best to help her through a time of female mystery.

She was gaining weight but she told herself it was only the baby, and would leave with its birth. But at other times she knew quite clearly that she was losing the discipline she had fought so hard to gain during her last year with Carrie. She was hungry now as she had been in college, and she ate between meals and after dinner and tried to eat only carrots and celery, but she grew to hate them, and her desire for sweets was as vicious as it had been long ago. At home she ate bread and jam and when she shopped for groceries she bought a candy bar and ate it driving home and put the wrapper in her purse and then in the garbage can under the sink. Her cheeks had filled out, there was loose flesh under her chin, her arms and legs were plump, and her mother was concerned. So was Richard. One night when she brought pie and milk to the living room where they were watching television, he said: "You already had a piece. At dinner."

She did not look at him.

"You're gaining weight. It's not all water, either. It's fat. It'll be summertime. You'll want to get into your bathing suit."

The pie was cherry. She looked at it as her fork cut through it; she speared the piece and rubbed it in the red juice on the plate before lifting it to her mouth.

"You never used to eat pie," he said. "I just think you ought to watch it a bit. It's going to be tough on you this summer."

In her seventh month, with a delight reminiscent of climbing the stairs to Richard's apartment before they were married, she returned to her world of secret gratification. She began hiding candy in her underwear drawer. She ate it during the day and at night while Richard slept, and at breakfast she was distracted, waiting for him to leave.

She gave birth to a son, brought him home, and nursed both him and her appetites. During this time of celibacy she enjoyed her body through her son's mouth; while he suckled she stroked his small head and back. She was hiding candy but she did not conceal her other indulgences: she was smoking again but still she ate between meals, and at dinner she ate what Richard did, and coldly he watched her, he grew petulant, and when the date marking the end of their celibacy came they let it pass. Often in the afternoons her mother visited and scolded her and Louise sat looking at the baby and said nothing until finally, to end it, she promised to diet. When her mother and father came for dinners, her father kissed her and held the baby and her mother said nothing about Louise's body, and her voice was tense. Returning from work in the evenings Richard looked at a soiled plate and glass on the table beside her chair as if detecting traces of infidelity, and at every dinner they fought.

"Look at you," he said. "Lasagna, for God's sake. When are you going to start? It's not simply that you haven't lost any weight. You're gaining. I can see it. I can feel it when you get in bed. Pretty soon you'll weigh more than I do and I'll be sleeping on a trampoline."

"You never touch me anymore."

"I don't want to touch you. Why should I? Have you *looked* at yourself?"

"You're cruel," she said. "I never knew how cruel you were."

She ate, watching him. He did not look at her. Glaring at his plate, he worked with fork and knife like a hurried man at a lunch counter.

"I bet you didn't either," she said.

That night when he was asleep she took a Milky Way to the bathroom. For a while she stood eating in the dark, then she turned on the light. Chewing, she looked at herself in the mirror; she looked at her eyes and hair. Then she stood on the scales and looking at the numbers between her feet, one hundred and sixty-two, she remembered when she had weighed a hundred and thirty-six pounds for eight days. Her memory of those eight days was fond and amusing, as though she were recalling an Easter egg hunt when she was six. She stepped off the scales and pushed them under the lavatory and did not stand on them again.

It was summer and she bought loose dresses and when Richard took friends out on the boat she did not wear a bathing suit or shorts; her friends gave her mischievous glances, and Richard did not look at her. She stopped riding on the boat. She told them she wanted to stay with the baby, and she sat inside holding him until she heard the boat leave the wharf. Then she took him to the front lawn and walked with him in the shade of the trees and talked to him about the blue jays and mockingbirds and cardinals she saw on their branches. Sometimes she stopped and watched the boat out on the lake and the friend skiing behind it.

Every day Richard quarrelled, and because his rage went no further than her weight and shape, she felt excluded from it, and she remained calm within layers of flesh and spirit, and watched his frustration, his impotence. He truly believed they were arguing about her weight. She knew better: she knew that beneath the argument lay the question of who Richard was. She thought of him smiling at the wheel of his boat, and long ago courting his slender girl, the daughter of his partner and friend. She thought of Carrie telling her of smelling chocolate in the dark and, after that, watching her eat it night after night. She smiled at Richard, teasing his anger.

He is angry now. He stands in the center of the living room, raging at her, and he wakes the baby. Beneath Richard's voice she hears the soft crying, feels it in her heart, and quietly she rises from her chair and goes upstairs to the child's room and takes him from the crib. She brings him to the living room and sits holding him in her lap, pressing him gently against the folds of fat at her waist. Now Richard is pleading with her. Louise thinks tenderly of Carrie broiling meat and fish in their room, and walking with her in the evenings. She wonders if Carrie still has the malaise. Perhaps she will come for a visit. In Louise's arms now the boy sleeps.

"I'll help you," Richard says. "I'll eat the same things you eat."

But his face does not approach the compassion and determination and love she had seen in Carrie's during what she now recognizes as the worst year of her life. She can remember nothing about that year except hunger, and the meals in her room. She is hungry now. When she puts the boy to bed she will get a candy bar from her room. She will eat it here, in front of Richard. This room will be hers soon. She considers the possibilities: all these rooms and the lawn where she can do whatever she wishes. She knows he will leave soon. It has been in his eyes all summer. She stands, using one hand to pull herself out of the chair. She carries the boy to his crib, feels him against her large breasts, feels that his sleeping body touches her soul. With a surge of vindication and relief she holds him. Then she kisses his forehead and places him in the crib. She goes to the bedroom and in the dark takes a bar of candy from her drawer. Slowly she descends the stairs. She knows Richard is waiting but she feels his departure so happily that, when she enters the living room, unwrapping the candy, she is surprised to see him standing there.

DELIVERING

Jimmy woke before the alarm, his parents' sounds coming back to him as he had known they would when finally three hours ago he knew he was about to sleep: their last fight in the kitchen, and Chris sleeping through it on the top bunk, grinding his teeth. It was nearly five now, the room sunlit; in the dark while they fought Jimmy had waited for the sound of his father's slap, and when it came he felt like he was slapping her and he waited for it again, wished for it again, but there was only the one clap of hand on face. Soon after that, she drove away.

Now he was ashamed of the slap. He reached down to his morning hardness which always he had brought to the bathroom so she wouldn't see the stain; he stopped once to turn off the alarm when he remembered it was about to ring into his quick breath. Then he stood and gently shook Chris's shoulder. He could smell the ocean. He shook Chris harder: twelve years old and chubby and still clumsy about some things. Maybe somebody else was Chris's father. No. He would stay with what he heard last night; he would not start making up more. Somewhere his mother was naked with that son of a bitch, and he squeezed Chris's shoulder and said: "Wake up." Besides, their faces looked alike: his and Chris's and his father's. Everybody said that. Chris stared at him.

"Come with me."

"You're crazy."

"I need you to."

"You didn't say anything last night."

"Come on."

"You buying the doughnuts?"

"After we swim."

In the cool room they dressed for the warm sun, in cut-off jeans and T-shirts and sneakers, and went quietly down the hall, past the closed door where Jimmy stopped and waited until he could hear his father's breath. Last night after she left, his father cried in the kitchen. Chris stood in the doorway, looking into the kitchen; Jimmy looked over his head at the table, the beer cans, his father's bent and hers straight, the ashtray filled, ashes on the table and, on the counter near the sink, bent cans and a Seagram's Seven bottle.

"Holy shit," Chris said.

"You'd sleep through World War III."

He got two glasses from the cupboard, reaching over the cans and bottle, holding his breath against their smell; he looked at the two glasses in the sink, her lipstick on the rim of one, and Chris said: "What's the matter?"

"Makes me sick to smell booze in the morning."

Chris poured the orange juice and they drank with their backs to the table. Jimmy picked up her Winston pack. Empty. Shit. He took a Pall Mall. He had learned to smoke by watching her, had started three years ago by stealing hers. He was twelve then. Would he and Chris see her alone now, or would they have to go visit her at that son of a bitch's house, wherever it was? They went out the back door and around to the front porch where the stacked papers waited, folded and tied, sixty-two of them, and a note on top saying Mr. Thompson didn't get his paper yesterday. "It's his Goddamn dog," he said, and cut the string and gave Chris a handful of rubber bands. Chris rolled and banded the papers while Jimmy stood on the lawn, smoking; he looked up the road at the small houses, yellow and brown and grey, all of them quiet with sleeping families, and the tall woods beyond them and, across the road, houses whose back lawns ended at the salt marsh that spread out to the northeast where the breeze came from. When he heard the rolling papers stop, he turned to Chris sitting on the porch and looking at him.

"Where's the car?"

"Mom took it."

"This early?"

He flicked the cigarette toward the road and kneeled on the porch and started rolling.

"Where'd she go so early?"

"Late. Let's go."

He trotted around the lawn and pushed up the garage door and went around the pickup; he did not look at Chris until he had unlocked the chain and pulled it from around the post, coiled it under his bicycle seat, and locked it there. His hands were ink-stained.

"You can leave your chain. We'll use mine at the beach."

He took the canvas sack from its nail on the post and hung it from his right side, its strap over his left shoulder, and walked his bicycle past the truck and out into the sun. At the front porch he stuffed the papers into the sack. Then he looked at Chris.

"We're not late," Chris said.

"She left late. Late last night." He pushed down his kickstand. "Hold on. Let's get these papers out."

"She left?"

"Don't you start crying on me. Goddamnit, don't."

Chris looked down at his handlebar.

"They had a fight," Jimmy said.

"Then she'll be back."

"Not this time. She's fucking somebody."

Chris looked up, shaking his head. Shaking it, he said: "No."

"You want to hear about it or you just going to stand there and tell me I didn't hear what I heard."

"Okay, tell me."

"Shit. I was going to tell you at the beach. Wait, okay?"

"Sixty-two papers?"

"You know she's gone. Isn't that enough for a while?" He kicked up his stand. "Look. We've hardly ever lived with both of them. It'll be like Pop's aboard ship. Only it'll be her."

"That's not true."

"What's not."

"About hardly ever living with both of them."

"It almost is. Let's go."

Slowly across the grass, then onto the road, pumping hard, shifting gears, heading into the breeze and sun, listening for cars to their rear, sometimes looking over his shoulder at the road and Chris's face, the sack bumping his right thigh and sliding forward but he kept shoving it back, keeping the rhythm of his pedalling and his throws: the easy ones to the left, a smooth motion across his chest like second to first, snapping the paper hard and watching it drop on the lawn; except for the people who didn't always pay on time or who bitched at him, and he hit their porches or front doors, a good hard sound in the morning quiet. He liked throwing to his right better. The first week or so he had cheated, had angled his bicycle toward the houses and thrown overhand; but then he stopped that, and rode straight, leaning back and throwing to his right, sometimes having to stop and leave his bicycle and get a paper from under a bush or a parked car in the driveway, but soon he was hitting the grass just before the porch, unless it was a house that had a door or wall shot coming, and he could do that with velocity too. Second to short. He finished his road by scaring himself, hitting Reilly's big front window instead of the wall beside it, and it shook but didn't break and when he turned his bicycle and headed back he grinned at Chris, who still looked like someone had just punched him in the mouth.

He went left up a climbing road past a pine grove, out of its shade into the warmth on his face: a long road short on customers, twelve of them scattered, and he rode faster, thinking of Chris behind him, pink-cheeked, breathing hard. Ahead on the right he saw Thompson's collie waiting on the lawn, and he pulled out a paper and pushed the sack behind his leg, then rose from the seat pumping toward the house, sitting as he left the road and bounced on earth and grass: he threw the paper thumping against the open jaws, his front tire gazing the yelping dog as it scrambled away, and he lightly hand-braked for his turn then sped out to the road again. He threw two more to his left and started up a long steep hill for the last of the route: the road cut through woods, in shade now, standing, the bicycle slowing as the hill steepened near the hardest house of all: the Claytons' at the top of the hill, a pale green house with a deep front lawn: riding on the shoulder, holding a paper against the handlebar, standing, his legs hot and tight, then at the top he sat to throw, the bicycle slowing, leaning, and with his left hand he moved the front wheel from side to side while he twisted to his right and cocked his arm and threw; he stood on the pedals and gained balance and speed before the paper landed sliding on the walk. The road wound past trees and fifteen customers and twice that many houses. He finished quickly. Then he got off his bicycle, sweating, and folded the sack and put it in his orange nylon saddlebag, and they started back, Chris riding beside him.

From one house near the road he smelled bacon. At another he saw a woman at the kitchen window, her head down, and he looked away. Some of the papers were inside now. At Clayton's house he let the hill take him down into the shade to flat land and, Chris behind him now, he rode past the wide green and brown salt marsh, its grass leaning with the breeze that was cool and sea-tanged on his face, moving the hair at his ears. There were no houses. A fruit and vegetable stand, then the bridge over the tidal stream: a quick blue flow, the tide coming in from the channel and cove beyond a bend to the north, so he could not see them, but he knew how the cove looked this early, with green and orange charter boats tied at the wharves.

An hour from now, the people would come. He and Chris and his father went a few afternoons each summer, with sandwiches and soft drinks and beer in the ice chest, and his father drank steadily but only a six-pack the whole afternoon, and they stood abreast at the rail, always near the bow, the boat anchored a mile or two out, and on lucky days filled a plastic bag with mackerel slapping tails till they died, and on unlucky ones he still loved the gentle rocking of the boat and the blue sea and the sun warmly and slowly burning him. Twice in late summer they had bottom-fished and pulled up cusks from three hundred feet, tired arm turning the reel, cusk breaking the surface with eyes pushed outward and guts in its mouth. His mother had gone once. She had not complained, had pretended to like it, but next time she told them it was too much sun, too smelly, too long. Had she been with that son of a bitch when they went fishing again? The boats headed in at five and his father inserted a cleaning board into a slot in the gunwale and handed them slick cool mackerel and he and Chris cleaned them and threw their guts and heads to the sea gulls that hovered and cried and dived until the boat reached the wharf. Sometimes they could make a gull come down and take a head from their fingers.

They rode past beach cottages and up a one-block street to the long dune that hid the sea, chained their bicycles to a telephone pole, and sprinted over loose sand and up the dune; then walking, looking at the empty beach and sea and breakers, stopping to take off sneakers and shirts, Jimmy stuffing his three bills into a sneaker, then running onto wet hard sand, into the surf cold on his feet and ankles, Chris beside him, and they both shouted at once, at the cold but to the sea as well, and ran until the water pushed at their hips and they walked out toward the sea and low sun, his feet hurting in the cold. A wave came and they turned their backs to it and he watched over his shoulder as it rose; when it broke they dived and he was riding it fast, swallowing water, and in that instant of old sea-panic he saw his father crying; he opened his eyes to the sting, his arms stretched before him, hands joined, then he was lying on the sand and the wave was gone and he stood shouting: "All *right*." They ran back into the sea and body-surfed until they were too cold, then walked stiffly up to higher sand. He lay on his back beside his clothes, looked at the sky; soon people would come with blankets and ice chests. Chris lay beside him. He shut his eyes.

"I was listening to the ball game when they came home. With the ear plug. They won, three to two. Lee went all the way. Rice drove in two with a double—" Bright field and uniforms under the lights in Oakland, him there too while he lay on his bunk, watching Lee working fast, Remy going to his left and diving to knock it down, on his knees for the throw in time when they came in talking past the door and down the hall to the kitchen "—They talked low for a long time; that's when they were drinking whiskey and mostly I just heard Pop getting ice, then I don't know why but after a while I knew it was trouble, all that ice and quiet talk and when they popped cans I figured they'd finished the whiskey and they were still talking that way so I started listening. She had already told him. That's what they were talking about. Maybe she told him at the Chief's Club. She was talking nice to him—"

"What did she say?"

"She said—shit—" He opened his eyes to the blue sky, closed them again, pressed his legs into the warm sand, listened to the surf. "She said I've tried to stop seeing him. She said Don't you believe I've tried? You think I want to hurt you? You know what it's like. I can't stop. I've tried and I can't. I wish I'd never met him. But I can't keep lying and sneaking around. And Pop said Bullshit: you mean you can't keep living here when you want to be fucking him. They didn't say anything for a minute and they popped two more cans, then she said You're right. But maybe I don't have to leave. Maybe if you'd just let me go to him when I wanted to. That's when he started yelling at her. They went at it for a long time, and I thought you'd wake up. I turned the game up loud as I could take it but it was already the ninth, then it was over, and I couldn't stop hearing them anyway. She said Jason would never say those things to her, that's all I know about that son of a bitch, his name is Jason and he's a civilian somewhere and she started yelling about all the times Pop was aboard ship he must have had a lot of women and who did he think he was anyway and she'd miss you and me and it broke her heart how much she'd miss you and me but she had to get out from under his shit, and he was yelling about she was probably fucking every day he was at sea for the whole twenty years and she said You'll never know you bastard you can just think about it for another twenty. That's when he slapped her."

"Good."

"Then she cried a little, not much, then they drank some more beer and talked quiet again. He was trying to make up to her, saying he was sorry he hit her and she said it was her fault, she shouldn't have said that, and she hadn't fucked anybody till Jason—"

"She said that?"

"What."

"Fuck."

"Yes. She was talking nice to him again, like he was a little kid, then she went to their room and packed a suitcase and he went to the front door with her, and I couldn't hear what they said. She went outside and he did too and after she drove off he came back to the kitchen and drank beer." He raised his head and looked past his feet at a sea gull bobbing on the water beyond the breakers. "Then he cried for a while. Then he went to bed."

"He did?"

"Yes."

"I've never heard him cry."

"Me neither."

"Why didn't you wake me up?"

"What for?"

"I don't know. I wish you had."

"I did. This morning."

"What's going to happen?"

"I guess she'll visit us or something."

"What if they send Pop to sea again and we have to go live with her and that guy?"

"Don't be an asshole. He's retiring and he's going to buy that boat and we'll fish like bastards. I'm going to catch a big fucking tuna and sell it to the Japanese and buy you some weights."

He squeezed Chris's bicep and rose, pulling him up. Chris turned his face, looking up the beach. Jimmy stepped in front of him, still holding his arm.

"Look: I heard Pop cry last night. For a long time. Loud. That's all the fucking crying I want to hear. Now let's take another wave and get some doughnuts."

They ran into the surf, wading coldly to the wave that rose until there was no horizon, no sea, only the sky beyond it.

Dottie from tenth grade was working the counter, small and summer-brown.

"Wakefield boys are here," Jimmy said. "Six honey dip to go."

He only knew her from math and talking in the halls, but the way she smiled at him, if it were any other morning, he would stay and talk, and any other day he would ask her to meet him in town tonight and go on some of the rides, squeeze her on the roller coaster, eat pizza and egg rolls at the stands, get somebody to buy them a six-pack, take it to the beach. He told her she was foxy, and got a Kool from her. Cars were on the roads now, but so many that they were slow and safe, and he and Chris rode side by side on the shoulder; Chris held the doughnut bag against the handlebar and ate while Jimmy smoked, then he reached over for the bag and ate his three. When they got near the house it looked quiet. They chained their bicycles in the garage and crept into the kitchen and past the closed door, to the bathroom. In the shower he pinched Chris's gut and said: "No shit, we got to work on that."

They put on gym shorts and sneakers and took their gloves and ball to the backyard.

"When we get warmed up I'm going to throw at your face, okay?"

"Okay."

"You're still scared of it there and you're ducking and you'll get hurt that way."

The new baseball smooth in his hand and bright in the sun, smacking in Chris's glove, coming back at him, squeezed high in the pocket and webbing; then he heard the back door and held the ball and watched his father walking out of the shade into the light. He squinted at his father's stocky body and sunburned face and arms, his rumpled hair, and motioned to Chris and heard him trotting on the grass. He was nearly as tall as his father, barely had to tilt his head to look into his eyes. He breathed the smell of last night's booze, this morning's sleep.

"I heard you guys last night," he said. "I already told him."

His father's eyes shifted to Chris, then back.

"She'll come by tomorrow, take you boys to lunch." He scratched his rump, looked over his shoulder at the house, then at Jimmy. "Maybe later we'll go eat some lobsters. Have a talk."

"We could cook them here," Chris said.

"Sure. Steamers too. Okay: I'll be out in a minute."

They watched him walk back to the house, then Jimmy touched Chris, gently pushed him, and he trotted across the lawn. They threw fly balls and grounders and one-hop throws from the outfield and straight ones to their bare chests, calling to each other, Jimmy listening to the quiet house too, seeing it darker in there, cooler, his father's closet where in a corner behind blue and khaki uniforms the shotgun leaned. He said, "Here we go," and threw at Chris's throat, then face, and heard the back door; his breath quickened, and he threw hard: the ball grazed the top of Chris's glove and struck his forehead and he bent over, his bare hand rubbing above his eye, then he was crying deeply and Jimmy turned to his running father, wearing his old glove, hair wet and combed, smelling of after-shave lotion, and said: "He's all right, Pop. He's all right."

A FATHER'S STORY

My name is Luke Ripley, and here is what I call my life: I own a stable of thirty horses, and I have young people who teach riding, and we board some horses too. This is in northeastern Massachusetts. I have a barn with an indoor ring, and outside I've got two fenced-in rings and a pasture that ends at a woods with trails. I call it my life because it looks like it is, and people I know call it that, but it's a life I can get away from when I hunt and fish, and some nights after dinner when I sit in the dark in the front room and listen to opera. The room faces the lawn and the road, a two-lane country road. When cars come around the curve northwest of the house, they light up the lawn for an instant, the leaves of the maple out by the road and the hemlock closer to the window. Then I'm alone again, or I'd appear to be if someone crept up to the house and looked through a window: a big-gutted grey-haired guy, drinking tea and smoking cigarettes, staring out at the dark woods across the road, listening to a grieving soprano.

My real life is the one nobody talks about anymore, except Father Paul LeBoeuf, another old buck. He has a decade on me: he's sixty-four, a big man, bald on top with grey at the sides; when he had hair, it was black. His face is ruddy, and he jokes about being a whiskey priest, though he's not. He gets outdoors as much as he can, goes for a long walk every morning, and hunts and fishes with me. But I can't get him on a horse anymore. Ten years ago I could badger him into a trail ride; I had to give him a western saddle, and he'd hold the pommel and bounce through the woods with me, and be sore for days. He's looking at seventy with eyes that are younger than many I've seen in people in their twenties. I do not remember ever feeling the way they seem to; but I was lucky, because even as a child I knew that life would try me, and I must be strong to endure, though in those early days I expected to be tortured and killed for my faith, like the saints I learned about in school.

Father Paul's family came down from Canada, and he grew up speaking more French than English, so he is different from the Irish priests who abound up here. I do not like to make general statements, or even to hold general beliefs, about people's blood, but the Irish do seem happiest when they're dealing with misfortune or guilt, either their own or somebody else's, and if you think you're not a victim of either one, you can count on certain Irish priests to try to change your mind. On Wednesday nights Father Paul comes to dinner. Often he comes on other nights too, and once, in the old days when we couldn't eat meat on Fridays, we bagged our first ducks of the season on a Friday, and as we drove home from the marsh, he said: For the purposes of Holy Mother Church, I believe a duck is more a creature of water than land, and is not rightly meat. Sometimes he teases me about never putting anything in his Sunday collection, which he would not know about if I hadn't told him years ago. I would like to believe I told him so we could have philosophical talk at dinner, but probably the truth is I suspected he knew, and I did not want him to think I so loved money that I would not even give his church a coin on Sunday. Certainly the ushers who pass the baskets know me as a miser.

I don't feel right about giving money for buildings, places. This starts with the Pope, and I cannot respect one of them till he sells his house and everything in it, and that church too, and uses the money to feed the poor. I have rarely, and maybe never, come across saintliness, but I feel certain it cannot exist in such a place. But I admit, also, that I know very little, and maybe the popes live on a different plane and are tried in ways I don't know about. Father Paul says his own church, St. John's, is hardly the Vatican. I like his church: it is made of wood, and has a simple altar and crucifix, and no padding on the kneelers. He does not have to lock its doors at night. Still it is a place. He could say Mass in my barn. I know this is stubborn, but I can find no mention by Christ of maintaining buildings, much less erecting them of stone or brick, and decorating them with pieces of metal and mineral and elements that people still fight over like barbarians. We had a Maltese woman taking riding lessons, she came over on the boat when she was ten, and once she told me how the nuns in Malta used to tell the little girls that if they wore jewelry, rings and bracelets and necklaces, in purgatory snakes would coil around their fingers and wrists and throats. I do not believe in frightening children or telling them lies, but if those nuns saved a few girls from devotion to things, maybe they were right. That Maltese woman laughed about it, but I noticed she wore only a watch, and that with a leather strap.

The money I give to the church goes in people's stomachs, and on their backs, down in New York City. I have no delusions about the worth of what I do, but I feel it's better to feed somebody than not. There's a priest in Times Square giving shelter to runaway kids, and some Franciscans who run a bread line; actually it's a morning line for coffee and a roll, and Father Paul calls it the continental breakfast for winos and bag ladies. He is curious about how much I am sending, and I know why: he guesses I send a lot, he has said probably more than tithing, and he is right; he wants to know how much because he believes I'm generous and good, and he is wrong about that; he has never had much money and does not know how easy it is to write a check when you have everything you will ever need, and the figures are mere numbers, and represent no sacrifice at all. Being a real Catholic is too hard; if I were one, I would do with my house and barn what I want the Pope to do with his. So I do not want to impress Father Paul, and when he asks me how much, I say I can't let my left hand know what my right is doing.

He came on Wednesday nights when Gloria and I were married, and the kids were young; Gloria was a very good cook (I assume she still is, but it is difficult to think of her in the present), and I liked sitting at the table with a friend who was also a priest. I was proud of my handsome and healthy children. This was long ago, and they were all very young and cheerful and often funny, and the three boys took care of their baby sister, and did not bully or tease her. Of course they did sometimes, with that excited cruelty children are prone to, but not enough so that it was part of her days. On the Wednesday after Gloria left with the kids and a U-Haul trailer, I was sitting on the front steps, it was summer, and I was watching cars go by on the road, when Father Paul drove around the curve and into the driveway. I was ashamed to see him because he is a priest and my family was gone, but I was relieved too. I went to the car to greet him. He got out smiling, with a bottle of wine, and shook my hand, then pulled me to him, gave me a quick hug, and said: "It's Wednesday, isn't it? Let's open some cans."

With arms about each other we walked to the house, and it was good to know he was doing his work but coming as a friend too, and I thought what good work he had. I have no calling. It is for me to keep horses.

In that other life, anyway. In my real one I go to bed early and sleep well and wake at four forty-five, for an hour of silence. I never want to get out of bed then, and every morning I know I can sleep for another four hours, and still not fail at any of my duties. But I get up, so have come to believe my life can be seen in miniature in that struggle in the dark of morning. While making the bed and boiling water for coffee, I talk to God: I offer Him my day, every act of my body and spirit, my thoughts and moods, as a prayer of thanksgiving, and for Gloria and my children and my friends and two women I made love with after Gloria left. This morning offertory is a habit from my boyhood in a Catholic school; or then it was a habit, but as I kept it and grew older it became a ritual. Then I say the Lord's Prayer, trying not to recite it, and one morning it occurred to me that a prayer, whether recited or said with concentration, is always an act of faith.

I sit in the kitchen at the rear of the house and drink coffee and smoke and watch the sky growing light before sunrise, the trees of the woods near the barn taking shape, becoming single pines and elms and oaks and maples. Sometimes a rabbit comes out of the treeline, or is already sitting there, invisible till the light finds him. The birds are awake in the trees and feeding on the ground, and the little ones, the purple finches and titmice and chickadees, are at the feeder I rigged outside the kitchen window; it is too small for pigeons to get a purchase. I sit and give myself to coffee and tobacco, that get me brisk again, and I watch and listen. In the first year or so after I lost my family, I played the radio in the mornings. But I overcame that, and now I rarely play it at all. Once in the mail I received a questionnaire asking me to write down everything I watched on television during the week they had chosen. At the end of those seven days I wrote in *The Wizard of Oz* and returned it. That was in winter and was actually a busy week for my television, which normally sits out the cold months without once warming up. Had they sent the questionnaire during baseball season, they would have found me at my set. People at the stables talk about shows and performers I have never heard of, but I cannot get interested; when I am in the mood to watch television, I go to a movie or read a detective novel. There are always good detective novels to be found, and I like remembering them next morning with my coffee.

I also think of baseball and hunting and fishing, and of my children. It is not painful to think about them anymore, because even if we had lived together, they would be gone now, grown into their own lives, except Jennifer. I think of death too, not sadly, or with fear, though something like excitement does run through me, something more quickening than the coffee and tobacco. I suppose it is an intense interest, and an outright distrust: I never feel certain that I'll be here watching birds eating at tomorrow's daylight. Sometimes I try to think of other things, like the rabbit that is warm and breathing but not there till twilight. I feel on the brink of something about the life of the senses, but either am not equipped to go further or am not interested enough to concentrate. I have called all of this thinking, but it is not, because it is unintentional; what I'm really doing is feeling the day, in silence, and that is what Father Paul is doing too on his five-to-ten-mile walks.

When the hour ends I take an apple or carrot and I go to the stable and tack up a horse. We take good care of these horses, and no one rides them but students, instructors, and me, and nobody rides the horses we board unless an owner asks me to. The barn is dark and I turn on lights and take some deep breaths, smelling the hay and horses and their manure, both fresh and dried, a combined odor that you either like or you don't. I walk down the wide space of dirt between stalls, greeting the horses, joking with them about their quirks, and choose one for no reason at all other than the way it looks at me that morning. I get my old English saddle that has smoothed and darkened through the years, and go into the stall, talking to this beautiful creature who'll swerve out of a canter if a piece of paper blows in front of him, and if the barn catches fire and you manage to get him out he will, if he can get away from you, run back into the fire, to his stall. Like the smells that surround them, you either like them or you don't. I love them, so am spared having to try to explain why. I feed one the carrot or apple and tack up and lead him outside, where I mount, and we go down the driveway to the road and cross it and turn northwest and walk then trot then canter to St. John's.

A few cars are on the road, their drivers looking serious about going to work. It is always strange for me to see a woman dressed for work so early in the morning. You know how long it takes them, with the makeup and hair and clothes, and I think of them waking in the dark of winter or early light of other seasons, and dressing as they might for an evening's entertainment. Probably this strikes me because I grew up seeing my father put on those suits he never wore on weekends or his two weeks off, and so am accustomed to the men, but when I see these women I think something went wrong, to send all those dressed-up people out on the road when the dew hasn't dried yet. Maybe it's because I so dislike getting up early, but am also doing what I choose to do, while they have no choice. At heart I am lazy, yet I find such peace and delight in it that I believe it is a natural state, and in what looks like my laziest periods I am closest to my center. The ride to St. John's is fifteen minutes. The horses and I do it in all weather; the road is well plowed in winter, and there are only a few days a year when ice makes me drive the pickup. People always look at someone on horseback, and for a moment their faces change and many drivers and I wave to each other. Then at St. John's, Father Paul and five or six regulars and I celebrate the Mass.

Do not think of me as a spiritual man whose every thought during those twenty-five minutes is at one with the words of the Mass. Each morning I try, each morning I fail, and know that always I will be a creature who, looking at Father Paul and the altar, and uttering prayers, will be distracted by scrambled eggs, horses, the weather, and memories and daydreams that have nothing to do with the sacrament I am about to receive. I can receive, though: the Eucharist, and also, at Mass and at other times, moments and even minutes of contemplation. But I cannot achieve contemplation, as some can; and so, having to face and forgive my own failures, I have learned from them both the necessity and wonder of ritual. For ritual allows those who cannot will themselves out of the secular to perform the spiritual, as dancing allows the tongue-tied man a ceremony of love. And, while my mind dwells on breakfast, or Major or Duchess tethered under the church eave, there is, as I take the Host from Father Paul and place it on my tongue and return to the pew, a feeling that I am thankful I have not lost in the forty-eight years since my first

Communion. At its center is excitement; spreading out from it is the peace of certainty. Or the certainty of peace. One night Father Paul and I talked about faith. It was long ago, and all I remember is him saying: Belief is believing in God; faith is believing that God believes in you. That is the excitement, and the peace; then the Mass is over, and I go into the sacristy and we have a cigarette and chat, the mystery ends, we are two men talking like any two men on a morning in America, about baseball, plane crashes, presidents, governors, murders, the sun, the clouds. Then I go to the horse and ride back to the life people see, the one in which I move and talk, and most days I enjoy it.

It is late summer now, the time between fishing and hunting, but a good time for baseball. It has been two weeks since Jennifer left, to drive home to Gloria's after her summer visit. She is the only one who still visits; the boys are married and have children, and sometimes fly up for a holiday, or I fly down or west to visit one of them. Jennifer is twenty, and I worry about her the way fathers worry about daughters but not sons. I want to know what she's up to, and at the same time I don't. She looks athletic, and she is: she swims and runs and of course rides. All my children do. When she comes for six weeks in summer, the house is loud with girls, friends of hers since childhood, and new ones. I am glad she kept the girl friends. They have been young company for me and, being with them, I have been able to gauge her growth between summers. On their riding days, I'd take them back to the house when their lessons were over and they had walked the horses and put them back in the stalls, and we'd have lemonade or Coke, and cookies if I had some, and talk until their parents came to drive them home. One year their breasts grew, so I wasn't startled when I saw Jennifer in July. Then they were driving cars to the stable, and beginning to look like young women, and I was passing out beer and ashtrays and they were talking about college.

When Jennifer was here in summer, they were at the house most days. I would say generally that as they got older they became quieter, and though I enjoyed both, I sometimes missed the giggles and shouts. The quiet voices, just low enough for me not to hear from wherever I was, rising and failing in proportion to my distance from them, frightened me. Not that I believed they were planning or recounting anything really wicked, but there was a female seriousness about them, and it was secretive, and of course I thought: love, sex. But it was more than that: it was womanhood they were entering, the deep forest of it, and no matter how many women and men too are saying these days that there is little difference between us, the truth is that men find their way into that forest only on clearly marked trails, while women move about in it like birds. So hearing Jennifer and her friends talking so quietly, yet intensely, I wanted very much to have a wife.

But not as much as in the old days, when Gloria had left but her presence was still in the house as strongly as if she had only gone to visit her folks for a week. There were no clothes or cosmetics, but potted plants endured my neglectful care as long as they could, and slowly died; I did not kill them on purpose, to exorcise the house of her, but I could not remember to water them. For weeks, because I did not use it much, the house was as neat as she had kept it, though dust layered the order she had made. The kitchen went first: I got the dishes in and out of the dishwasher and wiped the top of the stove, but did not return cooking spoons and pot holders to their hooks on the wall, and soon the burners and oven were caked with spillings, the refrigerator had more space and was spotted with juices. The living room and my bedroom went next; I did not go into the children's rooms except on bad nights when I went from room to room and looked and touched and smelled, so they did not lose their order until a year later when the kids came for six weeks. It was three months before I ate the last of the food Gloria had cooked and frozen: I remember it was a beef stew, and very good. By then I had four cookbooks, and was boasting a bit, and talking about recipes with the women at the stables, and looking forward to cooking for Father Paul. But I never looked forward to cooking at night only for myself, though I made myself do it; on some nights I gave in to my daily temptation, and took a newspaper or detective novel to a restaurant. By the end of the second year, though, I had stopped turning on the radio as soon as I woke in the morning, and was able to be silent and alone in the evening too, and then I enjoyed my dinners.

It is not hard to live through a day, if you can live through a moment. What creates despair is the imagination, which pretends there is a future, and insists on predicting millions of moments, thousands of days, and so drains you that you cannot live the moment at hand. That is what Father Paul told me in those first two years, on some of the bad nights when I believed I could not bear what I had to: the most painful loss was my children, then the loss of Gloria, whom I still loved despite or maybe because of our long periods of sadness that rendered us helpless, so neither of us could break out of it to give a hand to the other. Twelve years later I believe ritual would have healed us more quickly than the repetitious talks we had, perhaps even kept us healed. Marriages have lost that, and I wish I had known then what I know now, and we had performed certain acts together every day, no matter how we felt, and perhaps then we could have subordinated feeling to action, for surely that is the essence of love. I know this from my distractions during Mass, and during everything else I do, so that my actions and feelings are seldom one. It does happen every day, but in proportion to everything else in a day, it is rare, like joy. The third most painful loss, which became second and sometimes first as months passed, was the knowledge that I could never marry again, and so dared not even keep company with a woman.

On some of the bad nights I was bitter about this with Father Paul, and I so pitied myself that I cried, or nearly did, speaking with damp eyes and breaking voice. I believe that celibacy is for him the same trial it is for me, not of the flesh, but the spirit: the heart longing to love. But the difference is he chose it, and did not wake one day to a life with thirty horses. In my anger I said I had done my service to love and chastity, and I told him of the actual physical and spiritual pain of practicing rhythm: nights of striking the mattress with a fist, two young animals lying side by side in heat, leaving the bed to pace, to smoke, to curse, and too passionate to question, for we were so angered and oppressed by our passion that we could see no further than our loins. So now I understand how people can be enslaved for generations before they throw down their tools or use them as weapons, the form of their slavery—the cotton fields, the shacks and puny cupboards and untended illnesses—absorbing their emotions and thoughts until finally they have little or none at all to direct with clarity and energy at the owners and legislators. And I told him of the trick of passion and its slaking: how during what we had to believe were safe periods, though all four children were conceived at those times, we were able with some coherence to question the tradition and reason and justice of the law against birth control, but not with enough conviction to soberly act against it, as though regular satisfaction in bed tempered our revolutionary as well as our erotic desires. Only when abstinence drove us hotly away from each other did we receive an urge so strong it lasted all the way to the drugstore and back; but always, after release, we threw away the remaining condoms; and after going through this a few times, we knew what would happen, and from then on we submitted to the calendar she so precisely marked on the bedroom wall. I told him that living two lives each month, one as celibates, one as lovers, made us tense and short-tempered, so we snapped at each other like dogs.

To have endured that, to have reached a time when we burned slowly and could gain from bed the comfort of lying down at night with one who loves you and whom you love, could for weeks on end go to bed tired and peacefully sleep after a kiss, a touch of the hands, and then to be thrown out of the marriage like a bundle from a moving freight car, was unjust, was intolerable, and I could not or would not muster the strength to endure it. But I did, a moment at a time, a day, a night, except twice, each time with a different woman and more than a year apart, and this was so long ago that I clearly see their faces in my memory, can hear the pitch of their voices, and the way they pronounced words, one with a Massachusetts accent, one midwestern, but I feel as though I only heard about them from someone else. Each rode at the stables and was with me for part of an evening; one was badly married, one divorced, so none of us was free. They did not understand this Catholic view, but they were understanding about my having it, and I remained friends with both of them until the married one left her husband and went to Boston, and the divorced one moved to Maine. After both those evenings, those good women, I went to Mass early while Father Paul was still in the confessional, and received his absolution. I did not tell him who I was, but of course he knew, though I never saw it in his eyes. Now my longing for a wife comes only once in a while, like a cold: on some late afternoons when I am alone in the barn, then I lock up and walk to the house, daydreaming, then suddenly look at it and see it empty, as though for the first time, and all at once I'm weary and feel I do not have the energy to broil meat, and I think of driving to a restaurant, then shake my head and go on to the house, the refrigerator, the oven; and some mornings when I wake in the dark and listen to the silence and run my hand over the cold sheet beside me; and some days in summer when Jennifer is here.

Gloria left first me, then the Church, and that was the end of religion for the children, though on visits they went to Sunday Mass with me, and still do, out of a respect for my life that they manage to keep free of patronage. Jennifer is an agnostic, though I doubt she would call herself that, any more than she would call herself any other name that implied she had made a decision, a choice, about existence, death, and God. In truth she tends to pantheism, a good sign, I think; but not wanting to be a father who tells his children what they ought to believe, I do not say to her that Catholicism includes pantheism, like onions in a stew. Besides, I have no missionary instincts and do not believe everyone should or even could live with the Catholic faith. It is Jennifer's womanhood that renders me awkward. And womanhood now is frank, not like when Gloria was twenty and there were symbols: high heels and cosmetics and dresses, a cigarette, a cocktail. I am glad that women are free now of false modesty and all its attention paid the flesh; but, still, it is difficult to see so much of your daughter, to hear her talk as only men and bawdy women used to, and most of all to see in her face the deep and unabashed sensuality of women, with no tricks of the eyes and mouth to hide the pleasure she feels at having a strong young body. I am certain, with the way things are now, that she has very happily not been a virgin for years. That does not bother me. What bothers me is my certainty about it, just from watching her walk across a room or light a cigarette or pour milk on cereal.

She told me all of it, waking me that night when I had gone to sleep listening to the wind in the trees and against the house, a wind so strong that I had to shut all but the lee windows, and still the house cooled; told it to me in such detail and so clearly that now, when she has driven the car to Florida, I remember it all as though I had been a passenger in the front seat, or even at the wheel. It started with a movie, then beer and driving to the sea to look at the waves in the night and the wind, Jennifer and Betsy and Liz. They drank a beer on the beach and wanted to go in naked but were afraid they would drown in the high surf. They bought another six-pack at a grocery store in New Hampshire, and drove home. I can see it now, feel it: the three girls and the beer and the ride on country roads where pines curved in the wind and the big deciduous trees swayed and shook as if they might leap from the earth. They would have some windows partly open so they could feel the wind; Jennifer would be playing a cassette, the music stirring them, as it does the young, to memories of another time, other people and places in what is for them the past.

She took Betsy home, then Liz, and sang with her cassette as she left the town west of us and started home, a twenty-minute drive on the road that passes my house. They had each had four beers, but now there were twelve empty bottles in the bag on the floor at the passenger seat, and I keep focusing on their sound against each other when the car shifted speeds or changed directions. For I want to understand that one moment out of all her heart's time on earth, and whether her history had any bearing on it, or whether her heart was then isolated from all it had known, and the sound of those bottles urged it. She was just leaving the town, accelerating past a night club on the right, gaining speed to climb a long, gradual hill, then she went up it, singing, patting the beat on the steering wheel, the wind loud through her few inches of open window, blowing her hair as it did the high branches alongside the road, and she looked up at them and watched the top of the hill for someone drunk or heedless coming over it in part of her lane. She crested to an open black road, and there he was: a bulk, a blur, a thing running across her headlights, and she swerved left and her foot went for the brake and was stomping air above its pedal when she hit him, saw his legs and body in the air, flying out of her light, into the dark. Her brakes were screaming into the wind, bottles clinking in the fallen bag, and with the music and wind inside the car was his sound, already a memory but as real as an echo, that car-shuddering thump as though she had struck a tree. Her foot was back on the accelerator. Then she shifted gears and pushed it. She ejected the cassette and closed the window. She did not start to cry until she knocked on my bedroom door, then called: "Dad?"

Her voice, her tears, broke through my dream and the wind I heard in my sleep, and I stepped into jeans and hurried to the door, thinking harm, rape, death. All were in her face, and I hugged her and pressed her cheek to my chest and smoothed her blown hair, then led her, weeping, to the kitchen and sat her at the table where still she could not speak, nor look at me; when she raised her face it fell forward again, as of its own weight, into her palms. I offered tea and she shook her head, so I offered beer twice, then she shook her head, so I offered whiskey and she nodded. I had some rye that Father Paul and I had not finished last hunting season, and I poured some over ice and set it in front of her and was putting away the ice but stopped and got another glass and poured one for myself too, and brought the ice and bottle to the table where she was trying to get one of her long menthols out of the pack, but her fingers jerked like severed snakes, and I took the pack and lit one for her and took one for myself. I watched her shudder with her first swallow of rye, and push hair back from her face, it is auburn and gleamed in the overhead light, and I remembered how beautiful she looked riding a sorrel; she was smoking fast, then the sobs in her throat stopped, and she looked at me and said it, the words coming out with smoke: "I hit somebody. With the *car.*"

Then she was crying and I was on my feet, moving back and forth, looking down at her, asking *Who? Where? Where?* She was pointing at the wall over the stove, jabbing her fingers and cigarette at it, her other hand at her eyes, and twice in horror I actually looked at the wall. She finished the whiskey in a swallow and I stopped pacing and asking and poured another, and either the drink or the exhaustion of tears quieted her, even the dry sobs, and she told me; not as I tell it now, for that was later as again and again we relived it in the kitchen or living room, and, if in daylight, fled it on horseback out on the trails through the woods and, if at night, walked quietly around in the moonlit pasture, walked around and around it, sweating through our clothes. She told it in bursts, like she was a child again, running to me, injured from play. I put on boots and a shirt and left her with the bottle and her streaked face and a cigarette twitching between her fingers, pushed the door open against the wind, and eased it shut. The wind squinted and watered my eyes as I leaned into it and went to the pickup.

When I passed St. John's I looked at it, and Father Paul's little white rectory in the rear, and wanted to stop, wished I could as I could if he were simply a friend who sold hardware or something. I had forgotten my watch but I always know the time within minutes, even when a sound or dream or my bladder wakes me in the night. It was nearly two; we had been in the kitchen about twenty minutes; she had hit him around one-fifteen. Or her. The road was empty and

I drove between blowing trees; caught for an instant in my lights, they seemed to be in panic. I smoked and let hope play its tricks on me: it was neither man nor woman but an animal, a goat or calf or deer on the road; it was a man who had jumped away in time, the collision of metal and body glancing not direct, and he had limped home to nurse bruises and cuts. Then I threw the cigarette and hope both out the window and prayed that he was alive, while beneath that prayer, a reserve deeper in my heart, another one stirred: that if he were dead, they would not get Jennifer.

From our direction, east and a bit south, the road to that hill and the night club beyond it and finally the town is, for its last four or five miles, straight through farming country. When I reached that stretch I slowed the truck and opened my window for the fierce air; on both sides were scattered farmhouses and barns and sometimes a silo, looking not like shelters but like unsheltered things the wind would flatten. Corn bent toward the road from a field on my right, and always something blew in front of me: paper, leaves, dried weeds, branches. I slowed approaching the hill, and went up it in second, staring through my open window at the ditch on the left side of the road, its weeds alive, whipping, a mad dance with the trees above them. I went over the hill and down and, opposite the club, turned right onto a side street of houses, and parked there, in the leaping shadows of trees. I walked back across the road to the club's parking lot, the wind behind me, lifting me as I strode, and I could not hear my boots on pavement. I walked up the hill, on the shoulder, watching the branches above me, hearing their leaves and the creaking trunks and the wind. Then I was at the top, looking down the road and at the farms and fields; the night was clear, and I could see a long way; clouds scudded past the half-moon and stars, blown out to sea.

I started down, watching the tall grass under the trees to my right, glancing into the dark of the ditch, listening for cars behind me; but as soon as I cleared one tree, its sound was gone, its flapping leaves and rattling branches far behind me, as though the greatest distance

I had at my back was a matter of feet, while ahead of me I could see a barn two miles off. Then I saw her skid marks: short, and going left and downhill, into the other lane. I stood at the ditch, its weeds blowing; across it were trees and their moving shadows, like the clouds. I stepped onto its slope, and it took me sliding on my feet, then rump, to the bottom, where I sat still, my body gathered to itself, lest a part of me should touch him. But there was only tall grass, and I stood, my shoulders reaching the sides of the ditch, and I walked uphill, wishing for the flashlight in the pickup, walking slowly, and down in the ditch I could hear my feet in the grass and on the earth, and kicking cans and bottles. At the top of the hill I turned and went down, watching the ground above the ditch on my right, praying my prayer from the truck again, the first one, the one I would admit, that he was not dead, was in fact home, and began to hope again, memory telling me of lost pheasants and grouse I had shot, but they were small and the colors of their home, while a man was either there or not; and from that memory I left where I was and while walking in the ditch under the wind was in the deceit of imagination with Jennifer in the kitchen, telling her she had hit no one, or at least had not badly hurt anyone, when I realized he could be in the hospital now and I would have to think of a way to check there, something to say on the phone. I see now that, once hope returned, I should have been certain what it prepared me for: ahead of me, in high grass and the shadows of trees, I saw his shirt. Or that is all my mind would allow itself: a shirt, and I stood looking at it for the moments it took my mind to admit the arm and head and the dark length covered by pants. He lay face down, the arm I could see near his side, his head turned from me, on its cheek.

"Fella?" I said. I had meant to call, but it came out quiet and high, lost inches from my face in the wind. Then I said, "Oh God," and felt Him in the wind and the sky moving past the stars and moon and the fields around me, but only watching me as He might have watched Cain or Job, I did not know which, and I said it again, and wanted to sink to the earth and weep till I slept there in the weeds. I climbed, scrambling up the side of the ditch, pulling at clutched grass, gained the top on hands and knees, and went to him like that, panting, moving through the grass as high and higher than my face, crawling under that sky, making sounds too, like some animal, there being no words to let him know I was here with him now. He was long; that is the word that came to me, not tall. I kneeled beside him, my hands on my legs. His right arm was by his side, his left arm straight out from the shoulder, but turned, so his palm was open to the tree above us. His left cheek was clean-shaven, his eye closed, and there was no blood. I leaned forward to look at his open mouth and saw the blood on it, going down into the grass. I straightened and looked ahead at the wind blowing past me through grass and trees to a distant light, and I stared at the light, imagining someone awake out there, wanting someone to be, a gathering of old friends, or someone alone listening to music or painting a picture, then I figured it was a night light at a farmyard whose house I couldn't see. *Going*, I thought. *Still going*. I leaned over again and looked at dripping blood.

So I had to touch his wrist, a thick one with a watch and expansion band that I pushed up his arm, thinking *he's left-handed*, my three fingers pressing his wrist, and all I felt was my tough fingertips on that smooth underside flesh and small bones, then relief, then certainty. But against my will, or only because of it, I still don't know, I touched his neck, ran my fingers down it as if petting, then pressed, and my hand sprang back as from fire. I lowered it again, held it there until it felt that faint beating that I could not believe. There was too much wind. Nothing could make a sound in it. A pulse could not be felt in it, nor could mere fingers in that wind feel the absolute silence of a dead man's artery. I was making sounds again; I grabbed his left arm and his waist, and pulled him toward me, and that side of him rose, turned, and I lowered him to his back, his face tilted up toward the tree that was groaning, the tree and I the only sounds in the wind. Turning my face from his, looking down the length of him at his sneakers, I placed my ear on his heart, and heard not that but something else, and I clamped a hand over my exposed ear, heard something liquid and alive, like when you pump a well and after a few strokes you hear air and water moving in the pipe, and I knew I must raise his legs and cover him and run to a phone, while still I listened to his chest, thinking *raise with what? cover with what?* and amid the liquid sound I heard the heart, then lost it, and pressed my ear against bone, but his chest was quiet, and I did not know when the liquid had stopped, and do not know now when I heard air, a faint rush of it, and whether under my ear or at his mouth or whether I heard it at all. I straightened and looked at the light, dim and yellow. Then I touched his throat, looking him full in the face. He was blond and young. He could have been sleeping in the shade of a tree, but for the smear of blood from his mouth to his hair, and the night sky, and the weeds blowing against his head, and the leaves shaking in the dark above us.

I stood. Then I kneeled again and prayed for his soul to join in peace and joy all the dead and living; and, doing so, confronted my first sin against him, not stopping for Father Paul, who could have given him the last rites, and immediately then my second one, or I saw then, my first, not calling an ambulance to meet me there, and I stood and turned into the wind, slid down the ditch and crawled out of it, and went up the hill and down it, across the road to the street of houses whose people I had left behind forever, so that I moved with stealth in the shadows to my truck.

When I came around the bend near my house, I saw the kitchen light at the rear. She sat as I had left her, the ashtray filled, and I looked at the bottle, felt her eyes on me, felt what she was seeing too: the dirt from my crawling. She had not drunk much of the rye. I poured some in my glass, with the water from melted ice, and sat down and swallowed some and looked at her and swallowed some more, and said: "He's dead."

She rubbed her eyes with the heels of her hands, rubbed the cheeks under them, but she was dry now.

"He was probably dead when he hit the ground. I mean, that's probably what killed—"

"Where was he?"

"Across the ditch, under a tree."

"Was he—did you see his face?"

"No. Not really. I just felt. For life, pulse. I'm going out to the car."

"What for? Oh."

I finished the rye, and pushed back the chair, then she was standing too.

"I'll go with you."

"There's no need."

"I'll go."

I took a flashlight from a drawer and pushed open the door and held it while she went out. We turned our faces from the wind. It was like on the hill, when I was walking, and the wind closed the distance behind me: after three or four steps I felt there was no house back there. She took my hand, as I was reaching for hers. In the garage we let go, and squeezed between the pickup and her little car, to the front of it, where we had more room, and we stepped back from the grill and I shone the light on the fender, the smashed headlight turned into it, the concave chrome staring to the right, at the garage wall.

"We ought to get the bottles," I said.

She moved between the garage and the car, on the passenger side, and had room to open the door and lift the bag. I reached out, and she gave me the bag and backed up and shut the door and came around the car. We sidled to the doorway, and she put her arm around my waist and I hugged her shoulders.

"I thought you'd call the police," she said.

We crossed the yard, faces bowed from the wind, her hair blowing away from her neck, and in the kitchen I put the bag of bottles in the garbage basket. She was working at the table: capping the rye and putting it away, filling the ice tray, washing the glasses, empty-ing the ashtray, sponging the table.

"Try to sleep now," I said.

She nodded at the sponge circling under her hand, gathering ashes. Then she dropped it in the sink and, looking me full in the face, as I had never seen her look, as perhaps she never had, being for so long a daughter on visits (or so it seemed to me and still does: that until then our eyes had never seriously met), she crossed to me from the sink and kissed my lips, then held me so tightly I lost balance, and would have stumbled forward had she not held me so hard.

I sat in the living room, the house darkened, and watched the maple and the hemlock. When I believed she was asleep I put on *La Boheme*, and kept it at the same volume as the wind so it would not wake her. Then I listened to *Madame Butterfly*, and in the third act had to rise quickly to lower the sound: the wind was gone. I looked at the still maple near the window, and thought of the wind leaving farms and towns and the coast, going out over the sea to die on the waves. I smoked and gazed out the window. The sky was darker, and at daybreak the rain came. I listened to *Tosca*, and at six-fifteen went to the kitchen where Jennifer's purse lay on the table, a leather shoul-der purse crammed with the things of an adult woman, things she had begun accumulating only a few years back, and I nearly wept, thinking of what sandy foundations they were: driver's license, credit card, disposable lighter, cigarettes, checkbook, ballpoint pen, cash, cosmetics, comb, brush, Kleenex, these the rite of passage from child-hood, and I took one of them—her keys—and went out, remember-ing a jacket and hat when the rain struck me, but I kept going to the car, and squeezed and lowered myself into it, pulled the seat belt over my shoulder and fastened it and backed out, turning in the drive, going forward into the road, toward St. John's and Father Paul.

Cars were on the road, the workers, and I did not worry about any of them noticing the fender and light. Only a horse distracted them from what they drove to. In front of St. John's is a parking lot; at its far side, past the church and at the edge of the lawn, is an old pine, taller than the steeple now. I shifted to third, left the road, and, aiming the right headlight at the tree, accelerated past the white blur of church, into the black trunk growing bigger till it was all I could see, then I rocked in that resonant thump she had heard, had felt, and when I turned off the ignition it was still in my ears, my blood, and I saw the boy flying in the wind. I lowered my forehead to the wheel. Father Paul opened the door, his face white in the rain.

"I'm all right."

"What happened?"

"I don't know. I fainted."

I got out and went around to the front of the car, looked at the smashed light, the crumpled and torn fender.

"Come to the house and lie down."

"I'm all right."

"When was your last physical?"

"I'm due for one. Let's get out of this rain."

"You'd better lie down."

"No. I want to receive."

That was the time to say I want to confess, but I have not and will not. Though I could now, for Jennifer is in Florida, and weeks have passed, and perhaps now Father Paul would not feel that he must tell me to go to the police. And, for that very reason, to confess now would be unfair. It is a world of secrets, and now I have one from my best, in truth my only, friend. I have one from Jennifer too, but that is the nature of fatherhood.

Most of that day it rained, so it was only in early evening, when the sky cleared, with a setting sun, that two little boys, leaving their confinement for some play before dinner, found him. Jennifer and I got that on the local news, which we listened to every hour, meeting at the radio, standing with cigarettes, until the one at eight o'clock; when she stopped crying, we went out and walked on the wet grass, around the pasture, the last of sunlight still in the air and trees. His name was Patrick Mitchell, he was nineteen years old, was employed by CETA, lived at home with his parents and brother and sister. The paper next day said he had been at a friend's house and was walking home, and I thought of that light I had seen, then knew it was not for him; he lived on one of the streets behind the club. The paper did not say then, or in the next few days, anything to make Jennifer think he was alive while she was with me in the kitchen. Nor do I know if we—I—could have saved him.

In keeping her secret from her friends, Jennifer had to perform so often, as I did with Father Paul and at the stables, that I believe the acting, which took more of her than our daylight trail rides and our night walks in the pasture, was her healing. Her friends teased me about wrecking her car. When I carried her luggage out to the car on that last morning, we spoke only of the weather for her trip—the day was clear, with a dry cool breeze—and hugged and kissed, and I stood watching as she started the car and turned it around. But then she shifted to neutral and put on the parking brake and unclasped the belt, looking at me all the while, then she was coming to me, as she had that night in the kitchen, and I opened my arms.

I have said I talk with God in the mornings, as I start my day, and sometimes as I sit with coffee, looking at the birds, and the woods. Of course He has never spoken to me, but that is not something I require. Nor does He need to. I know Him, as I know the part of myself that knows Him, that felt Him watching from the wind and the night as I knelt over the dying boy. Lately I have taken to arguing with Him, as I can't with Father Paul, who, when he hears my monthly confession, has not heard and will not hear anything of failure to do all that one can to save an anonymous life, of injustice to a family in their grief, of deepening their pain at the chance and mystery of death by giving them nothing—no one—to hate. With Father Paul I feel lonely about this, but not with God. When I received the Eucharist while Jennifer's car sat twice-damaged, so redeemed, in the rain, I felt neither loneliness nor shame, but as though He were watching me, even from my tongue, intestines, blood, as I have watched my sons at times in their young lives when I was able to judge but without anger, and so keep silent while they, in the agony of their youth, decided how they must act; or found reasons, after their actions, for what they had done. Their reasons were never as good or as bad as their actions, but they needed to find them, to believe they were living by them, instead of the awful solitude of the heart.

I do not feel the peace I once did: not with God, nor the earth, or anyone on it. I have begun to prefer this state, to remember with fondness the other one as a period of peace I neither earned nor deserved. Now in the mornings while I watch purple finches driving larger titmice from the feeder, I say to Him: I would do it again. For when she knocked on my door, then called me, she woke what had flowed dormant in my blood since her birth, so that what rose from the bed was not a stable owner or a Catholic or any other Luke Ripley I had lived with for a long time, but the father of a girl.

And He says: I am a Father too.

Yes, I say, as You are a Son Whom this morning I will receive; unless You kill me on the way to church, then I trust You will receive me. And as a Son You made Your plea.

Yes, He says, but I would not lift the cup.

True, and I don't want You to lift it from me either. And if one of my sons had come to me that night, I would have phoned the police and told them to meet us with an ambulance at the top of the hill.

Why? Do you love them less?

I tell Him no, it is not that I love them less, but that I could bear the pain of watching and knowing my sons' pain, could bear it with pride as they took the whip and nails. But You never had a daughter and, if You had, You could not have borne her passion.

So, He says, you love her more than you love Me.

I love her more than I love truth.

Then you love in weakness, He says.

As You love me, I say, and I go with an apple or carrot out to the barn.

ALL THE TIME
IN THE WORLD

In college, LuAnn was mirthful and romantic, an attractive girl with black hair and dark skin and eyes. She majored in American Studies, and her discipline kept her on the dean's list. Her last name was Arceneaux; her mother's maiden name was Voorhies, and both families had come to Maine from Canada. Her parents and sister and brother and LuAnn often gestured with their hands as they talked. Old relatives in Canada spoke French.

LuAnn's college years seemed a fulfillment of her adolescence; she lived with impunity in a dormitory in Boston, with both girls and boys, with drinking and marijuana and cocaine; at the same time, she remained under the aegis of her parents. They were in a small town three hours north by bus; she went there on a few weekends, and during school vacations, and in summer. She was the middle child, between a married sister and a brother in high school. Her parents were proud of her work, they enjoyed her company, and they knew or pretended they knew as little about her life with friends as they had when she lived at home and walked a mile to school. In summer during college she was a lifeguard at a lake with a public beach. She saved some money and her parents paid her tuition and gave her a small allowance when she lived in the dormitory. They were neither strict nor lenient; they trusted her and, at home, she was like a young woman of their own generation: she drank and smoked with them, and on Sundays went to Mass with them and her brother. She went to Sunday Mass in Boston, too, and sometimes at noon on weekdays in the university chapel, and sitting in the pew she felt she was at home: that here, among strangers, she was all of herself, and only herself, forgiven and loved.

This was a time in America when courting had given way to passion, and passion burned without vision; this led to much postcoital intimacy, people revealing themselves to each other after they were lovers, and often they were frightened or appalled by what they heard as they were lying naked on a bed. Passion became smoke and left burned grass and earth on the sheets. The couple put on their clothes, fought for a few months, or tried with sincere and confessional negotiation to bring back love's blinding heat, then parted from each other and waited for someone else. While LuAnn was in college, she did not understand all of this, though she was beginning to, and she did not expect her parents to understand any of it. She secretly took birth control pills and, when she was at home, returned from dates early enough to keep at bay her parents' fears. At Mass she received Communion, her conscience set free by the mores of her contemporaries and the efficacy of the pill. When her parents spoke of drugs and promiscuity among young people, she turned to them an innocent face. This period of enjoying adult pleasures and at times suffering their results, while still living with her parents as a grown child, would end with the commencement she yearned for, strove for, and dreaded.

When it came, she found an apartment in Boston and a job with an insurance company. She worked in public relations. June that year was lovely, and some days she took a sandwich and cookies and fruit to work, and ate lunch at the Public Garden so she could sit in the sun among trees and grass. For the first time in her life she wore a dress or skirt and blouse five days a week, and this alone made her feel that she had indeed graduated to adult life. So did the work: she was assistant to a woman in her forties, and she liked the woman and learned quickly. She liked having an office and a desk with a telephone and typewriter on it. She was proud of her use of the telephone. Until now a telephone had been something she held while talking with friends and lovers and her family. At work she called people she did not know and spoke clearly in a low voice.

The office was large, with many women and men at desks, and she learned their names, and presented to them an amiability she assumed upon entering the building. Often she felt that her smiles, and her feigned interest in people's anecdotes about commuting and complaints about colds, were an implicit and draining part of her job. A decade later she would know that spending time with people and being unable either to speak from her heart or to listen with it was an imperceptible bleeding of her spirit.

Always in the office she felt that she was two people at once. She believed that the one who performed at the desk and chatted with other workers was the woman she would become as she matured, and the one she concealed was a girl destined to atrophy, and become a memory. The woman LuAnn worked for was an intense, voluble blonde who colored her hair and was cynical, humorous, and twice-divorced. When she spoke of money, it was with love, even passion; LuAnn saw money as currency to buy things with and pay bills, not an acquisition to accumulate and compound, and she felt like a lamb among wolves. The woman had a lover, and seemed happy.

LuAnn appreciated the practical function of insurance and bought a small policy on her own life, naming her parents as beneficiaries; she considered it a partial payment of her first child's tuition. But after nearly a year with the insurance company, on a Saturday afternoon while she was walking in Boston, wearing jeans and boots and a sweatshirt and feeling the sun on her face and hair, she admitted to herself that insurance bored her. Soon she was working for a small publisher. She earned less money but felt she was closer to the light she had sometimes lived in during college, had received from teachers and books and other students and often her own work. Now she was trying to sell literature, the human attempt to make truth palpable and delightful. There was, of course, always talk of money; but here, where only seven people worked and book sales were at best modest, money's end was much like its end in her own life: to keep things going. She was the publicity director and had neither assistants nor a secretary. She worked with energy and was not bored; still, there were times each day when she watched herself, and listened to herself, and the LuAnn Arceneaux she had known all her life wanted to say aloud: *Fuck* this; and to laugh.

She had lovers, one at a time; this had been happening since she was seventeen. After each one, when her sorrow passed and she was again resilient, she hoped for the next love; and her unspoken hope, even to herself, was that her next love would be her true and final one. She needed a name for what she was doing with this succession of men, and what she was doing was not clear. They were not affairs. An affair had a concrete parameter: the absence of all but physical love; or one of the lovers was married; or both of them were; or people from different continents met on a plane flying to a city they would never visit again; something hot and sudden like that. What LuAnn was doing was more complicated, and sometimes she called it naked dating: you went out to dinner, bared your soul and body, and in the morning went home to shower and dress for work. But she needed a word whose connotation was serious and deep, so she used the word everyone else used, and called it a relationship. It was not an engagement, or marriage; it was entered without vows or promises, but existed from one day to the next. Some people who were veterans of many relationships stopped using the word, and said things like: *I'm seeing Harry*, and *Bill and I are fucking*.

The men saw marriage as something that might happen, but not till they were well into their thirties. One, a tall, blond, curly-haired administrator at the insurance company, spoke of money; he believed a man should not marry until paying bills was no longer a struggle, until he was investing money that would grow and grow, and LuAnn saw money growing like trees, tulips, wild grass and vines. When she loved this man, she deceived herself and believed him. When she no longer loved him, she knew he was lying to her and to himself as well. Money had become a lie to justify his compromise of the tenderness and joy in his soul; these came forth when he was with her. At work he was ambitious and cold, spoke of precedent and the bottom line, and sometimes in the office she had to see him naked in her mind in order to see him at all.

One man she briefly loved, a sound engineer who wrote poems, regarded children as spiteful ingrates, fatherhood as bad for blood pressure, and monogamy as absurd. The other men she loved talked about marriage as a young and untried soldier might talk of war: sometimes they believed they could do it, and survive as well; sometimes they were afraid they could not; but it remained an abstraction that would only become concrete with the call to arms, the sound of drums and horns and marching feet. She knew with each man that the drumroll of pregnancy would terrify him; that even the gentlest—the vegetarian math teacher who would not kill the mice that shared his apartment—would gratefully drive her to an abortion clinic and tenderly hold her hand while she opened her legs. She knew this so deeply in her heart that it was hidden from her; it lay in the dark, along with her knowledge that she would die.

But her flesh knew the truth, and told her that time and love were in her body, not in a man's brain. In her body a man ejaculated, and the plastic in her uterus allowed him to see time as a line rising into his future, a line his lovemaking would not bend toward the curve of her body, the circle of love and time that was her womb and heart. So she loved from one day to the next, blinded herself to the years ahead, until hope was tired legs climbing a steep hill, until hope could no longer move upward or even stand aching in one flat and solid place. Then words came to her, and she said them to men, with derision, with anger, and with pain so deep that soon she could not say them at all, but only weep and, through the blur of tears, look at her lover's angry and chastened eyes. The last of her lovers before she met her final one was a carpenter with Greek blood, with dark skin she loved to see and touch; one night while they ate dinner in his kitchen, he called commitment "the *c* word." LuAnn was twenty-eight then. She rose from her chair, set down her glass of wine, and contained a scream while she pointed at him and said in a low voice: "You're not a man. You're a boy. You all are. You're all getting milk through the fence. You're a thief. But you don't have balls enough to take the cow."

This was in late winter, and she entered a period of abstinence, which meant that she stopped dating. When men asked her out, she said she needed to be alone for a while, that she was not ready for a relationship. It was not the truth. She wanted love, but she did not want her search for it to begin in someone's bed. She had been reared by both parents to know that concupiscence was at the center of male attention; she learned it soon enough anyway in the arms of frenzied boys. In high school she also learned that her passion was not engendered by a boy, but was part of her, as her blood and spirit were, and then she knew the words and actions she used to keep boys out of her body were also containing her own fire, so it would not spread through her flesh until its time. Knowing its time was not simple, and that is why she stopped dating after leaving the carpenter sitting at his table, glaring at her, his breath fast, his chest puffed with words that did not come soon enough for LuAnn to hear. She walked home on lighted sidewalks with gray snow banked on their curbs, and she did not cry. For months she went to movies and restaurants with women. On several weekends she drove to her parents' house, where going to sleep in her room and waking in it made her see clearly the years she had lived in Boston; made her feel that, since her graduation from college, only time and the age of her body had advanced, while she had stood on one plane, repeating the words and actions she regarded as her life.

On a Sunday morning in summer, she put on a pink dress and white high-heeled shoes and, carrying a purse, walked in warm sunlight to the ten o'clock Mass. The church was large and crowded. She did not know this yet, but she would in her thirties: the hot purity of her passion kept her in the Church. When she loved, she loved with her flesh, and to her it was fitting and right, and did not need absolving by a priest. So she had never abandoned the Eucharist; without it, she felt the Mass, and all of the Church, would be only ideas she could get at home from books; and because of it, she overlooked what was bureaucratic or picayune about the Church. Abortion was none of these; it was in the air like war. She hoped never to conceive a child she did not want, and she could not imagine giving death to a life in her womb. At the time for Communion she stepped into the line of people going to receive the mystery she had loved since childhood. A woman with gray hair was giving the Hosts; she took a white disk from the chalice, held it before her face, and said: "The Body of Christ." LuAnn said: "Amen," and the woman placed it in her palms and LuAnn put it in her mouth and for perhaps six minutes then, walking back to her pew and kneeling, she felt in harmony with the entire and timeless universe. This came to her every Sunday, and never at work; sometimes she could achieve it if she drove out of the city on a sunlit day and walked alone on a trail in woods, or on the shore of a lake.

After Mass she lingered on the church steps till she was alone. Few cars passed, and scattered people walked or jogged on the sidewalk, and a boy on a skateboard clattered by. She descended, sliding her hand down the smooth stone wall. A few paces from the steps, she turned her face up to the sun; then the heel of her left shoe snapped, and her ankle and knee gave way: she gained her balance and raised her foot and removed the broken shoe, then the other one. Her purse in one hand and her shoes in the other, she went to the steps and sat and looked at the heel hanging at an angle from one tiny nail whose mates were bent, silver in the sunlight. A shadow moved over her feet and up her legs and she looked at polished brown loafers and a wooden cane with a shining brass tip, and a man's legs in jeans, then up at his face: he had a trimmed brown beard and blue eyes and was smiling; his hair was brown and touched the collar of his navy blue shirt. His chest was broad, his waist was thick and bulged over his belt, and his bare arms were large; he said: "I could try to fix it."

"With what?"

He blushed, and said: "It was just a way of talking to you."

"I know."

"Would you like brunch?"

"Will they let me in barefoot?"

"When they see the shoe."

He held out his hand, and she took it and stood; her brow was the height of his chin. They told each other their names; he was Ted Briggs. They walked, and the concrete was warm under her bare feet. She told him he had a pretty cane, and asked him why.

"Artillery, in the war. A place called Khe Sanh."

"I know about Khe Sanh."

He looked at her.

"You do?"

"Yes."

"Good," he said.

"Why?"

"You were very young then."

"So were you."

"Nineteen."

"I was twelve."

"So how do you know about Khe Sanh?"

"I took a couple of courses. It's the best way to go to war."

He smiled, and said: "I believe it."

At a shaded corner they stopped to cross the street and he held her elbow as she stepped down from the curb. She knew he was doing this because of the filth and broken glass, and that he wanted to touch her, and she liked the feel of his hand. She liked the gentle depth of his voice, and his walk; his right knee appeared inflexible, but he walked smoothly. It was his eyes she loved; she could see sorrow in them, something old he had lived with, and something vibrant and solid, too. She felt motion in him, and she wanted to touch it. He was a lawyer; he liked to read and he liked movies and deep-sea fishing. On their left, cars stopped for a red light; he glanced at her, caught her gazing at his profile, and she said: "It was bad, wasn't it?"

He stopped and looked down at her.

"Yes. I was a corpsman. You know, the nurse, the EMT—" She nodded. "With the Marines. I got hurt in my twelfth month. Ten years later I started dealing with the eleven and a half months before that."

"How's it going?"

"Better. My knee won't bend, but my head is clear in the morning."

They walked; his hand with the cane was close to her left arm, and she could feel the air between their hands and wrists and forearms and biceps, a space with friction in it, and she veered slightly closer so their skin nearly touched. They reached the street where she lived and turned onto it, facing the sun, and she did not tell him this was her street. On the first block was the restaurant; she had walked or driven past it but had not been inside. He held the door for her and she went into the dark cool air and softened lights, the smells of bacon and liquor. She was on a carpet now, and she could see the shapes of people at tables, and hear low voices; then he moved to her right side, lightly placed his hand on her forearm, and guided her to a booth. They ordered: a Bloody Mary for her and orange juice for him, and cantaloupes and omelettes and Canadian bacon with English muffins. When their drinks came, she lit a cigarette and said: "I drink. I smoke. I eat everything."

"I go to meetings. I'm in my sixth year without a drink. My second without smoking." His hand came midway across the table. "But I'd love a hit off yours."

She gave him the cigarette, her fingers sliding under his. She left her hand there, waited for his fingers again, and got them, his knuckles beneath hers, and she paused for a moment before squeezing the cigarette and withdrawing her hand. She said: "Doesn't cheating make you miss it more?"

"Oh, I'm always missing something."

"Drinking?"

"Only being able to. Or thinking I was."

"Nothing horrible has ever happened to me."

"I hope nothing does."

"I suppose if I live long enough something will."

"If you don't live long enough, *that* would be horrible. Are you seeing anyone?"

"No. Are you?"

"No. I'm waiting. I limp. I get frightened suddenly, when there's no reason to be. I get sad too, when nothing has happened. I know its name now, and—"

"What is its name?"

"It. It's just it, and I go about my day or even my week sometimes, then it's gone. The way a fever is there, and then it isn't. I want a home with love in it, with a woman and children."

"My God," she said, and smiled, nearly laughing, her hands moving up from the table. "I don't think I've *ever* heard those words from the mouth of a man."

"I love the way you talk with your hands."

They stayed in the booth until midafternoon; he invited her to a movie that night; they stepped out of the restaurant into the bright heat, and he walked with her to the door of her apartment building, and stood holding her hand. She raised her bare heels and kissed his check, the hair of his beard soft on her chin, then went inside. She showered for a long time and washed her hair and, sitting at her mirror, blew it dry. She put on a robe and slept for an hour and woke happily. She ate a sandwich and soup, and dressed and put on makeup. He lived near the church, and he walked to her building and they walked to the movie; the sun was very low, and the air was cooling. After the movie he took her hand and held it for the four blocks to her apartment, where, standing on the sidewalk, he put his arms around her, the cane touching her right calf, and they kissed. She heard passing cars, and people talking as they walked by; then for a long time she heard only their lips and tongues, their breath, their moving arms and hands. Then she stepped away and said: "Not yet."

"That's good."

"You keep saying that."

"I keep meaning it."

He waited until she was inside both doors, and she turned and waved and he held up his hand till she was on the elevator, and she waved again as the door closed. In her apartment she went to her closet and picked up the white shoe with the broken heel. She did not believe in fate, but she believed in gifts that came; they moved with angels and spirits in the air, were perhaps delivered by them. Her red fingernails were lovely on the white leather; her hands warmed the heel.

In the morning she woke before the clock radio started, and made the bed; tonight she would see him. In her joy was fear, too, but it was a good fear of the change coming into her life. It had already come, she knew that; but she would yield slowly to it. She felt her months alone leaving her; she was shedding a condition; it was becoming her past. Outside in the sun, walking to work, she felt she could see the souls of people in their eyes. The office was bright; she could feel air touching her skin, and the warmth of electric lights.

With everyone she felt tender and humorous and patient, and happily mad. She worked hard, with good concentration, and felt this, too, molting: this trying to plunder from an empty cave a treasure for her soul. She went to lunch with two women, and ordered a steak and a beer. Her friends were amused; she said she was very hungry, and kept her silence.

What she had now was too precious and flammable to share with anyone. She knew that some night with Ted it would burst and blaze, and it would rise in her again and again, would course in her blood, burn in her face, shine in her eyes. And this time love was taking her into pain, yes, quarrels and loneliness and boiling rage; but this time there was no time, and love was taking her as far she would go, as long as she would live, taking her strongly and bravely with this Ted Briggs, holding his pretty cane; this man who was frightened by what had happened to him, but not by the madness she knew he was feeling now. She was hungry, and she talked with her friends and waited for her steak, and for all that was coming to her: from her body, from the earth, from radiant angels poised in the air she breathed.

A Note on the Text

The stories in *In the Bedroom* appear in the following Andre Dubus collections:

"Killings," "The Winter Father," "Rose," "The Fat Girl," "Delivering," and "A Father's Story" in *Selected Stories*; "All the Time in the World" in *Dancing After Hours*.